NATURE DETECTIVES

There was a loud rustle and the cub in the brambles came bounding out.

NATURE DETECTIVES

By

DONALD CUNNINGHAM

Illustrated by A. Burgess Sharrocks

LONDON

MACMILLAN & CO LTD

NEW YORK · ST MARTIN'S PRESS

1959

MACMILLAN AND COMPANY LIMITED
London Bombay Calcutta Madras Melbourne

THE MACMILLAN COMPANY OF CANADA LIMITED
Toronto

ST MARTIN'S PRESS INC
New York

PRINTED IN GREAT BRITAIN

CONTENTS

CHAPTER I

ROBERT MAKES A START

ROBERT ARMSTRONG was feeling excited as he and his father hurried into Waterloo Station. Robert had often met well-known detectives, for his father was a member of the C.I.D., but this time they were meeting Mr. John Thornley, the world-famous naturalist. They had often watched him on television, and Robert knew that his father had been at school with him many years ago, but he never expected to meet such a famous man face to face. However, two days ago Mr. Armstrong had received a letter from Mr. Thornley, and now they were about to meet him.

They pushed their way through the jostling crowds until they reached the barrier to Platform 12, where they waited. In a few minutes a West Country express came gliding in, and Mr. Arm-

I

strong scanned the scurrying throng with a practised eye. Suddenly he stepped forward, and Robert found himself gazing at the face he had seen so many times on the screen. It was a thin, weather-beaten, hawk-like face, which reminded Robert of a Red Indian.

The two men shook hands warmly and exchanged greetings. When this was done Mr. Armstrong introduced Robert.

" Ah—so this is Robert," said Mr. Thornley with a quick smile. " How are you, young man? "

What keen eyes he has, thought Robert, what a brown skin, and what a strong hand.

" Robert's keen on Nature," said Mr. Armstrong. " He never misses one of your films."

" I'm glad you like them," said Mr. Thornley, " but I think I should explain that Nature isn't half so exciting as it may seem on television. I've often spent hours in a hide for just one picture, and many times I've waited with cameras ready and seen nothing."

" Yes, I've done the same, sir," replied Robert. " I fixed up a hide in my friend's garden last Easter, and tried to get some photos of a blackbird at her nest."

" Did you get them? "

" No. I think the light was wrong, but I saw the bird come back and settle down on her eggs. I watched her shuffling her feathers in the way you showed in one of your films."

" Good. Don't scorn the common birds. There's a lot we don't know about blackbirds and sparrows."

" He used to spend all his spare time reading detective stories," said Mr. Armstrong, " but he seems to be more interested in Nature now."

" Well, there's a strong connection between the two. Every good naturalist has to be a bit of a detective. Come along—I'm not used to these crowds."

. . . . .

Robert's head was in a whirl when he went to bed that night. He had seen so many photographs of birds and animals that he could imagine owls sitting on the cupboard, and fox-cubs peeping out from under the bed. Mr. Thornley had a gift for making his stories come alive, so that Robert felt as if he had really seen the little foxes romping in the bracken, and the owl bringing mice to its fluffy owlets.

He switched off the light and lay awake for a long time, thinking. How he would love to investigate some of those mysteries about which Mr. Thornley had spoken. Bird migration, for instance. He had never realised how little was really known about Nature. The clock struck eleven before he finally fell asleep.

. . . . .

Robert was helping his mother to serve breakfast, and had just set down a heavy tray when the doorbell rang. He rushed to answer it, and there stood a telegraph-boy, holding out a small yellow envelope.

Robert took it. It was addressed to Mr. Thornley.

" Any answer? " asked the boy.

" Oh—wait a minute. I'll go and see," replied Robert. He turned and ran upstairs to Mr. Thornley's room, wondering what the telegram was about. He felt quite excited as he knocked at the door.

Mr. Thornley came to the door, and without a word tore open the envelope. Robert watched his face. It looked troubled.

" Is it bad news, sir? " asked Robert.

" Yes, I'm afraid it is." He glanced at Robert's anxious face and smiled. " Oh, not as bad as all that ! It simply says that my partner can't come photographing squirrels next week—which is going to be awkward at such short notice. . . . Tell the boy there's no reply—here—give him this." He handed Robert a sixpence.

The boy grinned when Robert gave him the coin. Lucky chap, thought Robert—getting sixpence just for waiting two minutes on somebody's doorstep. He pondered on whether he should change his mind and become a telegraph boy—dashing around the country on a red motor-bike and getting all those sixpences, which he could save up for a lovely country holiday. He was still thinking about it as the family sat down to breakfast.

" Yes, it's bad luck," said Mr. Armstrong, " but tell me, why is it so important to have an assistant? Couldn't you do it alone? "

" Not half so well. It's quite likely that nothing would come near the hide except animals that I didn't want to photograph."

" Why's that? "

" Well, the creature which you are going to photograph is usually watching you when you enter the hide, though you don't see it. If it sees you enter, it knows you are there, and won't come near. But if two of you enter—and after a few minutes one of you leaves— the creature thinks the coast is clear."

" Well—how quaint ! " said Mrs. Armstrong. " I suppose wild creatures don't know that two ones are two."

" That's it. They don't seem to study arithmetic," replied Mr. Thornley.

4

" Lucky things," murmured Robert.   Mr. Thornley smiled at
him.   Suddenly his face went serious and he stared hard.   Robert
felt awkward under that keen gaze.

" I wonder if it would work," murmured Mr. Thornley to
himself.

" Why, what do you mean? " asked Mr. Armstrong.

" Well, I need an assistant—and your son wants to do a bit of
nature-study—and his Easter holiday is just starting.   What do you
think? "

In the silence Robert could feel his heart thumping.   He stared at
his father.

" If you're prepared to take a chance with him—I won't say no,"
said Mr. Armstrong thoughtfully.

There was no need to ask Robert—his face was one big smile.

" Thanks awfully ! " he burst out.   " I'd simply love to come.
I'll be ever so quiet."

" Right—then it's settled.   You ask Mother to get your bag
packed tonight, and we'll start tomorrow."

.   .   .   .   .

" What do you know about grey squirrels? " asked Mr. Thornley
as they walked through the woods towards the hide.

" Well—I know they're not British.   They came from America,
didn't they? "

" That's right.   What else? "

" Oh—let's see—they drove away the red squirrels—and they
steal eggs—and kill young birds."

" Hm.   How do you know? "

" I read it in a book."

" Yes, that's just the trouble. You read it in a book," said Mr Thornley thoughtfully.

" What do you mean, sir? "

" It doesn't do to believe all the stuff one reads in books. I want to see if the grey squirrel is really such a rascal as he is painted."

" Don't you think he is? "

" Well, I have my doubts. You'll see why in a few minutes."

At the Keeper's Cottage they called to see if a helper was in They were lucky, for the Keeper himself was just starting off on his round of traps. He was a tall, thin man who spoke very softly, and always seemed to be listening for something.

" Yes, I'm coming your way, sir. No trouble at all, sir—though I'd shoot the lot if the Captain would give the word." He hitched his bag over his shoulder, picked up his gun, and joined them Robert noticed how quietly he walked, in spite of his size, and how his head turned from side to side, as he glanced at every bush and tree. " Like a Red Indian," thought Robert. He walked behind the two men, trying to copy the Keeper's movements, and feeling very proud to be one of the party.

Presently Mr. Thornley stopped, glanced round at Robert and raised a finger to his lips. Then he turned sharply off the main path and led the way up a steep bank. They had to bend low to avoid the hazel branches, which grew beneath the taller trees. Robert stepped on a dead stick which cracked, and the two men stopped and glared at him in silence.

" Sorry," whispered Robert. He felt his ears going red.

" Never step on sticks," said Mr. Thornley softly. " One dry stick cracking will scare every creature for a quarter of a mile."

6

They listened. There was no
sound but the singing of the birds.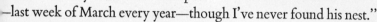
" Willow warbler's back, I see,"
said Mr. Thornley in a quiet tone.
The Keeper nodded.

"Ah. Always comes to this spot
—last week of March every year—though I've never found his nest."

" Can you hear it, Robert? " asked Mr. Thornley, raising one
black eyebrow in a curious manner.

" No, sir—I don't know many bird-songs," replied Robert.
How silly he felt ! But Mr. Thornley didn't seem in the least surprised.

" Listen. Up in that beech—a very shrill sweet song, like a fairy
coming down the scale ! "

Robert smiled at Mr. Thornley's description of the song. Then
he spotted a movement high up in the bare branches and saw a
tiny greenish-brown bird flitting rapidly from branch to branch,
and pecking here and there.

" Is that it? " he whispered.

" That's it—all the way from Africa."

The tiny bird sang again, shaking all over as it uttered its sweet
notes. It hardly paused in its feeding.

" I shall know that one again," said Robert.

" Excuse me, sir," said the Keeper quietly, " there's a pheasant's
nest in those brambles. Like to see it? "

" I never refuse a nest," replied Mr. Thornley.

The Keeper walked slowly forward, looking carefully at the trees.
Surely, thought Robert, pheasants nest on the ground ! The

7

Keeper stopped, looked left and right, and walked slowly forward again. Finally he stood quite still gazing intently at something on the ground. Then he beckoned.

"Softly," whispered Mr. Thornley

Robert found he was holding his breath as he tiptoed forward, trying to step over every bramble and dead leaf. He wondered why the two men could tread so lightly, while he seemed to make such a noise. As he reached the Keeper's side he caught sight of the pheasant, crouching quite still among the brambles. She was not hidden, but he would never have noticed her by himself, for her spotted brown feathers were just the same colour as the dead leaves and withered grass.

For a whole minute they stood watching. Robert noticed that the pheasant blinked her eye several times. Then the Keeper made one step forward. Instantly there was a frightful clatter, a hoarse cackling cry, and a furious beating of wings, as the bird rose into the air and went whirring away down the slope. Robert jumped, but the Keeper seemed not to have heard the noise at all. He was looking at the beautiful brown eggs with a puzzled frown.

"Drat it—there's two more gone. It's those urchins, I'll be bound, if it isn't a brock."

Mr. Thornley said nothing, but bent and examined the nest intently. He looked all round it, turning over dead leaves where they were thick, and stooping over patches of bare soil. Then he straightened his back and looked at the Keeper.

"I bet it's neither," he said.

8

" Take you on, sir," replied the Keeper.

" All right—but I shall have to trap the thief to prove it. Do you mind? "

" Not at all, sir."

Mr. Thornley noticed Robert's bewildered face and chuckled.

" All right, Robert—it's just our way of investigating a crime. Did you understand what we meant? "

" No, sir, I haven't a clue. And why did the Keeper look at the trees to find a nest on the ground? "

Mr. Thornley glanced at the Keeper.

" Well, son, it's like this," explained the Keeper. " When I find a nest I mark it, or I'd never find it again. To mark this 'un, I walk back to the birch, with the oak behind me. I count my steps— ten steps. Then I walk back to the path and mark the spot where I turned off—a thick bunch of honeysuckle. When I come again, I make for the birch, and then take ten steps towards the oak. You see? "

" Oh yes, I see. And what are those things you mentioned— brocks, and . . ."

" Brocks and urchins? They're just country names. Badgers and hedgehogs you'd call 'em."

" Do you think they've been robbing your nests? "

" I do—but Mr. Thornley's got other ideas."

" What do you think, Mr. Thornley? " asked Robert.

" Wait and see, my lad," said Mr. Thornley with a mysterious smile.

CHAPTER II

DETECTIVES IN HIDING

THEY were in the hide at last, and the Keeper's footsteps were dying away. Robert felt thrilled. How Tom Bradley and Richard Long would envy him if they could see him now, sitting on a camp-stool beside the famous naturalist. The hide was a square tent, made of dull brown canvas, and through a peep-hole Robert could see an open space among the trees. Half-way up an oak was a large untidy nest, made of branches with dead brown leaves still attached. " A drey," Mr. Thornley had whispered. Scattered on the ground was some maize, and as Robert looked more closely he noticed several small white objects lying here and there under the hazels.

" What are those white things ? " he whispered, as softly as he could.

Mr. Thornley's lips hardly moved as he answered, " Pigeons' eggs."

The minutes passed. Nothing happened but the movement of little birds, searching the branches for insects. Robert was determined not to become bored, and he began to examine every bush and tree. What was that yellowish splash on a tree-trunk, a little to the left? It looked like mud. Robert looked at Mr. Thornley, who grinned and raised a finger to his lips.

When Robert looked back at the tree, he noticed a movement on the trunk. A bird was clinging to the bark—a plump little bird with a bluish back and a rather long beak. Robert was screwing up his eyes and staring hard when a nudge from Mr. Thornley made him start, and there was a wonderful pair of field-glasses in his hands. When he raised them to his eyes, everything seemed to dance about as though he were in an aeroplane. At last he focused on the patch, and saw to his amazement that it really was yellow clay. It appeared to be about three yards away now, and he could see every detail clearly.

Robert kept the glasses steady and waited. Suddenly, there was the bird, holding a lump of clay in its beak.

It smacked its beak left, right, left, with quick jerky strokes, looked smartly round, and vanished.

" A nuthatch," whispered Mr. Thornley.

Back came the bird with another beakful of clay. Robert had never seen a bird with such unusual colours. Its back was bluish-grey, its breast brownish-red, and it had a thick black stripe running through its eye. When it paused for a sideways glance he noticed its strong, pointed beak. It clung to the rough bark like a wood-

B

pecker, its stubby tail pressed to the trunk. To and fro it flew, bringing more and more clay, which it slapped into the hole with such force that Robert wondered why it did not hurt itself.

" Quick! quick! quick!" Robert heard a clear shrill call ring out from somewhere overhead. The nuthatch paused and twisted its head to look up. It answered with the same call and flew away. Robert lowered the glasses and turned to Mr Thornley.

" What's it doing?" he whispered.

" The hole is too big," whispered Mr. Thornley, " so she fills it up with clay."

" But she won't be able to get in if she does that."

" Won't she? You just watch."

Robert watched the tree, but nothing stirred for several minutes He wondered if a nuthatch was the same as a woodpecker, and why it had such a strange name. Suddenly there was a flash of wings and the bird alighted on the vertical trunk. It climbed up to the hole in jerky hops. When it reached the hole it looked carefully from side to side, and then began to hammer fiercely at the centre of the clay. It worked with so much energy that it appeared to be fighting an unseen enemy. At short intervals it paused to rest, and then renewed the attack, until a hole appeared in the centre of the clay. The bird paused for a few moments and then set to work again, pecking rapidly here and there to shape the hole. Soon it was large enough for it to creep through, and it disappeared inside Then its head came out and a small object fell to the ground Robert guessed that it was throwing out the small pieces of clay which had fallen into the hole.

At last the nuthatch appeared to be satisfied. It poked its head out, called three times, and flew off.

Robert lowered the glasses and grinned at Mr. Thornley, who grinned back and raised his forefinger to signal " Silence ". Robert continued to scan the branches with his glasses. He had never realised before how many small birds there were in a wood. Great tits and blue tits were flitting from branch to branch, hunting busily for insects. There was another tit without the yellow breast of the first two, and there were some slim little greenish-brown birds which were quite unknown to him. He made up his mind to look them up in Mr. Thornley's book when he got back to the Fisherman's Rest. This was the name of the inn beside the river where he was staying with Mr. Thornley.

Presently he felt his arms aching and lowered the glasses. Mr. Thornley was staring intently at something higher up in the trees, and following his glance, Robert saw something flicking and jerking on a bough. It looked rather like a snake. Robert looked more closely, and suddenly the thing took shape—it was a squirrel, crouching quite still except for its jerking tail. It was staring hard at the drey. Suddenly it ran along the branch to the drey, but as it reached the untidy nest, another squirrel appeared from inside, making an angry chattering noise. In an instant the first squirrel turned and fled. When it reached the tip, the branch swayed and bent, and Robert clenched his hands, expecting the little animal to fall, but the squirrel took a flying leap on to the tip of another branch and raced along it to the trunk. The second squirrel followed in exactly the same way, and the two chased round and round the trunk, so that Robert could not see which was which.

Suddenly the chase ended. One squirrel came scrambling down the trunk head first, taking a leap when about four feet from the ground. It bounded along rather as a rabbit does, jerking its tail up and down with a wavy movement, and rustling loudly among the leaves. Then it began to nose about on the ground. Robert noticed that it was not grey all over, but quite brown on its sides, and its ears were round, not pointed, as he fancied he had seen in pictures.

A gentle nudge made him look up. Mr. Thornley was staring at a tree-trunk a little to the left. Clinging head downwards to the trunk was the other squirrel.

" Look at its hind feet," whispered Mr. Thornley.

Robert looked. The hind feet were pointing backwards—

even the toes—so that the claws hooked on to the rough bark. Robert had never seen any animal turn its hind feet back like this. He shifted his gaze to the front feet, and to his surprise they were not holding on to the tree at all, but were raised to the squirrel's nibbling jaws. It was just hanging by its hind feet.

" What's he eating?" whispered Mr. Thornley.

When Robert got the glasses focused and stopped the picture wobbling, the squirrel looked close enough to stroke. Its big shining eye seemed to stare right into his. Something green and crinkly was held between its hand-like paws, and as it nibbled it dropped little bits. Surely that wasn't a nut? Suddenly it dropped the last bit, and whisked round the trunk out of sight.

" It was something green," whispered Robert, as he lowered the glasses and watched the squirrel climb to a higher branch.

The squirrel ran along a branch till it swayed dangerously. It reached out on to such a thin twig that the twig began to bend, but just in time it drew back. In its mouth Robert could see a green tuft of half-opened leaves. It scampered back to a thicker branch, and this time it sat up on its hind legs in true picture-book fashion to nibble its food.

" Watch the other one," whispered Mr. Thornley.

The other squirrel was still nosing busily about on the ground, nibbling hard. When the one in the tree descended, and came bounding forwards, the first one made the queer chattering noise again and chased him off. Robert was wondering which was which when he heard Mr. Thornley's faint whisper in his ear.

" She's the female. I can tell her because she's a little larger than he is. She's got babies up there. She wants to bag all the maize for herself."

" Is he her mate? "

" I expect so—can't be sure. Look, she's finished the maize. See if she starts on the eggs."

The female sat up on her hind legs and peered about. Then she bounded across towards the right. She passed three eggs without appearing to notice them. She had just begun to nose about under the hazels when Robert was startled by a loud scuffling of leaves, and something rushed out from behind a fallen tree-trunk. There was a flash of whisking tails, and on the ground crouched an angry tabby cat, ears down, eyes glaring upwards, and tail lashing.

" Is it a wild cat? " whispered Robert.

" No, just a poaching cat. That nearly wrecked my experiment."

Both squirrels were making the funniest coughing noises, ending in a sort of squeal. Their tails were fluffed out like brushes, and jerking all the time. They gradually climbed higher and higher, while the cat glared up at them. Presently it turned and padded softly away. Then came another sound, a sharp clapping of wings, almost overhead, and a blue-and-white pigeon darted away through the tree-tops.

" Good," whispered Mr. Thornley, as he squinted up through a hole in the roof. " Just what I want."

" What is it? "

" See if you can spot it."

It was quite a while before Robert noticed a skimpy nest of dead sticks in the fork of a silver birch.

" Is that a pigeon's nest? "

" Yes, that's it. Now we'll see if the squirrels take the eggs."

" They didn't take them on the ground."

" No, but perhaps they don't recognize them on the ground. Hark—here comes a real egg-robber ! Keep quiet."

Robert had noticed nothing. He listened and then heard a harsh call, repeated three times. It sounded something like a rook. Mr. Thornley nodded and grinned.

A shadow skimmed across the clearing, and a large black bird landed heavily in one of the oaks. It looked around carefully, stretched its neck, and called again. There was a swish of wings, and a second black bird came swooping down beside it. Another careful glance all around, and the first bird dropped down, landing with a bounce in the dead leaves. It stared hard at the hide for several seconds, and then walked across to a pigeon's egg and snatched it up in its beak. As it sprang into the air Mr. Thornley clapped his hands and let out such a yell that Robert jumped with fright. There was a hoarse " craw " and both birds made off at top speed, while the egg dropped back on to the leaves and rolled into a hollow.

" Gosh—you made me jump ! " said Robert.

" Sorry, son—I had to scare them or they'd have upset my test completely. Wish I'd had a gun for once."

" What were they? "

" Crows—carrion crows—worst egg-thieves in the land. They'll snap up an egg anywhere."

" Do you think the squirrels get the blame for stealing eggs which crows take? "

" No doubt they often do."

" Did they steal the pheasants' eggs? "

" Can't say yet. Wait till we have some evidence. Well, we may as well go home for lunch now—we've scared everything away."

When they reached the Fisherman's Rest, Robert stopped to stare at a huge fish in a glass case. It looked simply enormous. Under the case was a notice, which said: " Caught by George Whiting Esq. on the 21st March 1936." Robert stood staring at the fish, and wondering how such a monster would look if it were swimming now.

" Interested in fishing, son? " asked Tom Wickenden, the landlord.

" Well, I've never done any proper fishing—I've only caught tiddlers with a home-made rod. I say—was that fish really caught here? "

" Ah, that it was! I remember how excited us young chaps were when old George landed that big fellow."

" He's a beauty all right," said Mr. Thornley, coming up behind them. " An old grandfather, by the look of that hooked jaw. Do you ever catch trout that size now? "

" Not now, sir," replied Tom. " Not since they're given up the Otter Hunt."

" Is that so, Tom? "

" That's how it is, sir. Those otters have all the big 'uns now." He shook his head sadly and walked away.

" I say, Mr. Thornley, is that right? " asked Robert. Mr. Thornley sighed.

" You see, Robert, this is what we're always up against. What would your Dad say if the Court condemned a suspect without trial? "

" He'd say it was jolly unjust, sir."

" Suppose the suspect was dumb, and couldn't defend himself? "

" Why, that would make it all the worse."

" Exactly ! "

" Do you mean it's the same about otters? "

" Not only otters. There are dozens of suspects—squirrels, badgers, hedgehogs, hawks, owls—in fact some people want to destroy nearly all our wild creatures on account of the harm which they are supposed to do."

They walked into the dining-room, and for several minutes neither of them spoke.

" I tell you what, sir," said Robert at last. " I'd like to be a sort of detective, like my Dad, only I'd investigate all these tales about animals and birds. I bet half of them aren't true."

" You're right, son. That's what we need—some first-class nature detectives."

CHAPTER III

BY THE RIVER

Mr. Thornley had promised Robert a walk by the river that evening. Robert was anxious to start straight away, but Mr. Thornley, like all grown-ups, had that maddening habit of saying, " It's not time yet—we needn't start till nearly seven."

Robert was leaving the room when his eye fell on Mr. Thornley's reference book on birds. Perhaps he could look up those little greenish-brown birds which he had seen from the hide.

" Excuse me, Mr. Thornley—please may I borrow that book?" asked Robert. "I want to look something up."

Mr. Thornley nodded and continued writing, so Robert picked up the book and began to scan the coloured plates. Presently he came across a picture which looked like the bird which he had seen. "Willow Warbler", it was called. He was about to show it to Mr. Thornley when he noticed another picture beside it. This bird looked exactly the same, but it was called " Chiff-chaff".

" Can I help? " asked Mr. Thornley.

Robert glanced up and realised that he was being watched.

" These two birds look exactly the same to me," he said, bringing the book to the table.

" Yes, they do to most bird-watchers. In fact, the only way you can be sure is to trap the bird and examine the wing. In the chiff-chaff the second primary feather is shorter than the sixth, and in the willow warbler it's the same length or longer. The primary feathers are those at the tip of the wing. The easiest way to tell which bird is which is to listen to the songs."

" What does the chiff-chaff sound like? " asked Robert. " I remember the willow warbler now."

" The chiff-chaff sings its own name, over and over again. It sounds like a pixie sharpening his scythe."

" Thanks," said Robert. " I'll try to remember that."

" You go and look for nests in the lane," said Mr. Thornley. " Come back just before seven, and we'll go for that walk."

Robert wandered off down the lane and searched for nests. He found a thrush's, a blackbird's, a chaffinch's and a queer little nest with one egg different from the rest. When he got back he walked quietly in, and heard the voices of Tom Wickenden and Mr. Thornley arguing. He listened.

"Vermin—that's what they are—vermin," Tom was saying. " Same as stoats and weasels. Same family, so I'm told. Only got to look at their teeth. I've seen many a cock trout left lying on the bank with just one bite out of his back. That's otter's work, isn't it? "

" True, true. But look here, Tom—would it surprise you if I told you that it might be better for the fishing if those old cock trout were removed from the river? "

" That seems nonsense to me. Fish has to have fathers, don't they, same as everything else? "

Mr. Thornley chuckled. " All right, Tom," he said quietly, " I'll say no more till I can prove my point."

Tom snorted. " Take chickens too," he complained. " Old

Charlie Bates lost five pullets last week—you know him : he lives in that cottage just below the bridge."

" Yes, I know.   His run is right beside the water, isn't it ?   What makes him think it was an otter ? "

" Well, the wire was a bit low on the side by the river.   Charlie didn't miss them till the end of the week, when he counted them. Then he found a place where the wire was pressed down, as though something had jumped over.   It was close to the water."

" I see—and he thinks that proves it was an otter."

" What else could it have been ?   A fox would have killed a whole lot and left them lying about—and a rat couldn't have dragged them up over that wire."

There was a pause.   Then Robert heard Mr. Thornley's voice. He sounded very serious.

" Look here, Tom—if Charlie will give me permission to set a trap, I'll see if I can catch the thief."

" Right, sir !   I'll ask him when he comes in this evening—and I'll take a bet that you'll catch an otter."

The telephone rang, and Tom went to answer it.   Mr. Thornley strolled into the passage.

" Another case for the nature detectives, sir ? " said Robert.

" Yes, looks like it, Robert."

" It isn't crows this time, is it ? "

" Now don't you start judging the accused before hearing the evidence.   You wait and see."

.   .   .   .   .

Birds were singing all around them as they walked quietly along beside the river, for the sun was almost setting.   They stopped to

ook at a thrush, which was singing noisily, and a little further on
they spotted a fine cock blackbird, singing in a hawthorn tree.
Robert noticed how soft and slow the blackbird's song sounded,
after the quick shrill notes of the thrush.

They stopped for a few minutes to listen. When the blackbird
paused in his song another blackbird could be heard on the far side of
the river. Mr. Thornley glanced at Robert to see if he had noticed.

The blackbird finished its song with a shrill squeak, and flew away
into the wood, but Mr. Thornley did not move. He was listening
to the other blackbird, which went on singing for a little longer.

" That's something about which we can only guess," he said.

" What do you mean, Mr. Thornley? "

" Bird-song. Have you ever stopped to consider why they sing? "

" No. I suppose they sing because they're happy."

Mr. Thornley smiled.

" Maybe. That's as good a theory as any I've heard."

" Well, why do they sing? " asked Robert.

" Most naturalists think that they sing to let others know that the area round their nest is occupied. It's like those notices you see in woods sometimes: 'Trespassers will be prosecuted'. They only sing regularly at nesting-time. You noticed that those two blackbirds appeared to be answering one another, didn't you? "

" Yes, I did notice that. You know, Mr. Thornley, I never realised before you came how many things in Nature are still not understood. I used to think that the experts had discovered everything."

" Not by a long way, Robert. Nature is full of unsolved mysteries. It's like your Dad's work in a way, but much less sordid. Take that bird, for instance."

He pointed to a fairly large bird with a long narrow tail, which was skimming steadily along just above the trees beyond the river.

" What is it? " asked Robert.

Mr. Thornley drew him behind a bush and, taking a deep breath, gave an excellent imitation of the call of a cuckoo. The bird turned instantly and flew straight towards them. It was almost over the bush before it saw them. Robert caught a glimpse of its yellow eyes and barred breast as it swerved sharply and made off.

" I say—that was clever," exclaimed Robert. " Will they always come like that when you call? "

" Not always, but it usually works in early Spring."

" Why do they come? "

" That's another thing I don't know. Perhaps it's the cock who comes, in answer to my challenge, or perhaps it's the hen who thinks I'm a cock."

" Have you ever found a cuckoo's egg? " asked Robert.

" Oh yes, many times. They're not so difficult to find. If you ever come across a small nest with one egg which is different from the rest——"

" Oh, Mr. Thornley, I found one this evening," exclaimed Robert. " It was in the hedge quite close to the Fisherman's Rest. The other eggs were blue, but this one had grey spots."

" That sounds like a cuckoo's egg in a hedge-sparrow's nest. Perhaps we shall be able to take some pictures of the young cuckoo."

" Why do cuckoos . . ." began Robert, but Mr. Thornley stopped him.

" Now, Robert, it's no use asking me. The cuckoo is one of Nature's biggest mysteries. We don't even know how it's done, let alone why. You could spend a lifetime studying cuckoos. Come along, we must find somewhere to hide, or we shall be too late to see anything."

Presently they came to a meadow where cows lay peacefully chewing the cud. The cows turned their heads as the two passed by, staring with their big brown curious eyes. Robert noticed that their breath looked like steam.

" Dew's falling," said Mr. Thornley. " It's going to be chilly by the water. It's a good job I made you bring your coat."

" Where are we stopping? " asked Robert.

For answer Mr. Thornley pointed to a big willow, standing on a little mound, with the river curving round on three sides. As they approached, Robert noticed that the trunk was hollow, with an opening on each side. They ducked their heads and entered.

" Find a comfortable seat," whispered Mr. Thornley. "You look out on that side and I'll look on this. Hallo—someone's been here." He was fingering a screwed-up newspaper, which smelt strongly of fish and chips. He paused thoughtfully, looking at the crumpled paper. Suddenly he glanced at Robert and smiled.

" This is where your detective training comes in handy. Think now—what sort of person would eat fish and chips inside this old tree? "

" It might be some people out for a picnic," suggested Robert.

" It might, but picnic parties aren't allowed here. Only fishermen are allowed here."

" Well, it might be a fisherman."

" I doubt it. Fishermen generally come for the whole day and bring their own food. Where would they get fish and chips in a quiet spot like this? "

" I don't know," replied Robert. " You've made it sound as mysterious as a detective story. Where would they get fish and chips? "

" There's a van which calls at the village once a week, on Fridays. Today is Wednesday. Let's look at the date on that paper."

He smoothed the crumpled paper on his knee.

" Look—the 20th April—that's last Wednesday, a week ago. I should say that this mysterious visitor was here last Friday evening."

" Why evening? "

" Because the van doesn't reach the village until about four o'clock. Who would come fishing in the evening, do you think? Not one of the regulars, surely."

" No. I should think it's somebody who isn't supposed to be here. Would it be a poacher? "

Mr. Thornley smiled.

" I think I could put my finger right on him," he said.

" I say—how on earth could you do that? "

" Didn't you notice a Gypsy caravan beside the lane as we were coming from the station? That caravan belongs to a family well known to me. They are old friends of mine. I expect this paper was left by young Luke. He's very fond of fishing."

" He'll get into trouble if he's caught, won't he? "

" Yes. I must get him a permit."

" I say, Mr. Thornley, did you say these Gypsies are friends of yours? " asked Robert in a puzzled tone.

" Yes. I've known them for years. They've given me many useful tips about where to find wild creatures. Once you make friends with a Gypsy, you have a friend for life."

Robert was thinking deeply, and did not speak for a minute.

" I should love to meet some Gypsies," he said at length.

" Perhaps you will. I'll see what I can do. No more talking now. Give me a poke if you see anything exciting."

For a long time all was quiet. The sun sank, a glowing orange ball, and for a time the beautiful colours of the sky were reflected in the smooth water. How peaceful it is, thought Robert. Birds were still singing, and now and then the watchers heard a splash as a fish jumped.

A bat appeared, flying up and down, up and down above the water. Sometimes it dropped about a foot and went flickering on again. Robert turned to Mr. Thornley.

" It's pouching an insect," whispered Mr. Thornley.

" Pouching it? "

" Yes—it curls its tail up to form a pouch. Can you hear it squeak? "

Robert listened. Yes, he could hear a faint fairy-like squeaking when it passed close. He nodded. They were both listening hard when the queerest sound was heard, a soft whistle, which echoed across the water. Three times it sounded, and then from upstream they heard a splash. Mr. Thornley turned to Robert with a delighted grin.

" Otters," he whispered.

Robert was staring hard at the water when he felt a gentle nudge, and turned his head to follow Mr. Thornley's gaze. What was that small creature creeping along in the grass? Was it a rat? No, it looked too big for a rat. It glided up to the dark shape of a cow, and Robert thought he heard a faint crunching sound.

Mr. Thornley opened his mouth to whisper, but stopped as a harsh scream rang out on the other side of the hide. Turning quickly, Robert caught sight of a huge bird circling round, with long legs dangling. The bird dropped gently down, landing with a faint splash in the shallow water where the river curved. As it stood, with its long neck stretched out, it looked exactly like a stork. Surely, he thought, there are no storks in England! Whatever could it be?

The minutes slipped by, and the bird stood as still as a statue. An owl hooted, a long quavering " Hooo! hoo-hoo-hoo-hoo! " Robert wondered why it was not getting any darker, but when he turned his head he saw the great round globe of the moon peeping over the tree-tops. He turned back to watch the bird. Its head

seemed to have moved, for now its beak was pointing at the water. Everything was as still as a picture. Would nothing happen? How long would the silly thing stand there?

Robert's thoughts began to wander. Fancy Mr. Thornley being friendly with a Gypsy family. Robert had always thought of Gypsies as lazy dishonest people. He had never realised that a man like Mr. Thornley might include Gypsies among his friends. Perhaps they knew things about wild creatures which were still unknown to the experts. Wouldn't it be exciting if he could get to know them, and find out some of their secrets?

He tried to imagine the boy Luke, whom Mr. Thornley had mentioned. He could not remember anything about Gypsies except that they were usually dark, and their clothes looked ragged and dirty. He was trying to imagine Luke creeping into the hollow tree when his day-dream was interrupted by a loud splash, for the bird had moved at last.

The long snaky neck shot down into the water, and now something was wriggling furiously, gripped by the sharp beak. The big bird twisted and turned its head this way and that, for the thing it held squirmed and shook. After a moment, the bird strode rapidly upstream, and Robert heard a dull "Thump, thump" as it beat its captive against something hard.

"Thump, thump, thump." Robert counted eighteen, then a pause, and then more blows. At length the bird raised its beak upwards and jerked it several times, as if changing its grip. Then it started swallowing, as Robert could see from the queer movements of the neck. It went on swallowing for about a minute, and Robert grinned as he thought how uncomfortable he would be if he had to gulp his meat down like this, all in one piece. At last it stopped swallowing and walked slowly back to its fishing-place, where it became still once more.

Robert was longing to ask questions. What was the bird, and what had it caught? He glanced at Mr. Thornley, who made no move. He was wondering whether he dared try a faint whisper when there came a swirl and a splash in the water. The big bird gave a harsh scream and sprang into the air with flapping wings, while a dark shape glided swiftly across the pool. The next moment something appeared on the bank—a long crouching animal, with a blunt head. It stood quite still for a few seconds, and then moved on till it reached a little knoll. Here it raised its head and stared in all directions. Robert could see its thick tail plainly, and knew that at last he was looking at an otter.

The otter lowered its head, and Robert heard a crunching sound. It was eating something. Suddenly a low whistle sounded —so close that it made Robert start. The otter raised its head again, paused for a moment, and glided down to the water. There was no splash—just a wide circle of ripples dying slowly away on the shining surface of the river.

Robert gave a loud sigh, for he had been holding his breath with excitement. He could see the outline of Mr. Thornley's face among the shadows, and he was smiling.

" You've seen it," came a faint whisper.

They waited in silence, but nothing happened. The owl hooted again, a long echoing call, and then Robert saw it, flying rather slowly and quite silently along the river-bank. It passed close by, like a huge moth, and all was still again. Robert began to feel cold, and when he moved his leg he found it had gone to sleep. " Pins and needles " started, and although he tried hard he could not keep his leg still.

" All right, son—let's go," said Mr. Thornley suddenly. His voice sounded shockingly loud after the long silence.

" Sorry, sir—it's pins and needles," mumbled Robert, rubbing the leg fiercely.

31

" I know—nasty feeling—but it soon goes. Next time, be very careful how you sit. Don't have your legs bent sharply, or crossed."

" Have you ever had it? "

" Oh yes, lots of times."

Mr. Thornley crawled out and walked towards the little knoll where the otter had rested. He stopped and picked something up. Robert saw the silvery gleam of a fish.

" Evidence," said Mr. Thornley.

" What sort, sir? " asked Robert as he reached his side.

" We'll see when we open its stomach. Now let's go quietly— we may see something on our way home."

As they reached the big hunched forms of the cows, Mr. Thornley suddenly gripped Robert's arm and pointed. There was the small animal again, scuttling away from one of the cows. Mr. Thornley broke into a trot, and came up with the little creature, which suddenly stopped running and lay still.

" What is it? " asked Robert.

For answer, Mr. Thornley took a torch from his pocket and shone it down into the grass. There was no mistaking that prickly ball.

" A hedgehog ! " cried Robert in surprise.

" That's it."

"What was it doing by the cows? "

" Tom would say it was sucking their milk."

Robert chuckled. " Wouldn't it look funny? " he said.

" Yes, wouldn't it—its mouth would be so wide open that it couldn't move its jaws to suck, and nobody has explained why the cows would put up with those sharp teeth pricking them."

" Well, what *was* it doing? "

By the River

" That's just what we don't know. Some say searching for beetles, which the cows squash or frighten away as they lie down; and some say just keeping warm. We must get more evidence before we can tell. But people suspect the worst, as usual."

" What was the big bird, Mr. Thornley? Was it a stork? "

" No, that was a heron—another one on Tom's black-list. But the funny thing is that it killed an eel, which destroys thousands of baby fish. That's something Tom hasn't thought of."

They walked quietly on. Moorhens were still calling, and now they heard wild ducks quacking from the meadows across the river. Presently there was a whistle of wings, and they saw five ducks fly over, long necks poking out ahead.

" Don't these birds ever sleep? " whispered Robert.

" Not on moonlight nights—and even on dark nights you can hear them about. I guess they sleep in snatches during the day."

" What a queer idea! Why don't they come out by day and sleep at night, like us? "

" Probably because for thousands of years they've been hunted by day, and they've found it safer to feed at night."

" What a pity ! " said Robert.

They walked on in silence, until the lighted windows of the Fisherman's Rest came in sight. The lights looked very cosy, but Robert was sorry to be back. As he sat by the fire drinking his cocoa, he kept thinking of the misty moonlit river, where unseen birds were splashing and calling, and otters glided beneath the shining water.

CHAPTER IV

A STUDY IN DETECTION

ROBERT was just dropping off to sleep when he was woken by a piercing cat-squall. He sat up with a start and heard it again. He jumped out of bed, ran to the window, and leaned out. Down below a door banged, and heavy footsteps ran towards the bridge. Then he heard an excited shout:

" You got him all right, sir! "

Next moment the crash of a gun made him jump with fright. What was happening? Was the inn being attacked by robbers? He rushed out into the passage, and stood listening at the top of the stairs. Presently he heard footsteps outside, the front door opened, and in walked Mr. Thornley and the landlord.

" Well, Tom, you've lost your bet! " said Mr. Thornley. He glanced up, and noticed Robert. " It's all right—it isn't burglars."

" What's happened? " asked Robert.

" We caught the thief who was stealing Charlie's pullets."

" Was it an otter? "

" No fear—or I shouldn't have won my bet. You get back to bed and I'll tell you all about it in the morning."

. . . . .

As soon as Robert was dressed, Mr. Thornley took him round to Charlie Bates's chicken-run.

" I laid a trap here," said Mr. Thornley, pointing to a spot just in

34

ront of the hen-house door, " and I left the door open. I intended
o get up at five o'clock and remove it if nothing was caught."

" But how did you know it wasn't an otter? " asked Robert.

Mr. Thornley smiled, and led the way round to the river-bank.

"An otter would land close to the run if he knew where to find
he birds. Now, you just show me where he landed, night after
ight."

1098574

Robert searched the bank from the bridge to the end of the garden,
ut never a trace of a track could he find.

" Is there any more evidence? " he asked.

" Yes—take a look at this." Mr. Thornley was stooping over a
muddy patch of soil, close to the run. Printed clearly in the mud
were two small impressions of animal's feet.

" See any claw-marks? " asked Mr. Thornley.

Robert shook his head.

"An otter would leave the marks of his claws, and perhaps his
webs. This is a cat's track. Charlie doesn't keep a cat, and he
hadn't noticed one about by day. The chances were that it came
by night. You see? "

" Poor thing," said Robert. " Still, you have proved it wasn't an
otter. Charlie might have shot an otter instead."

" If you ask me, Charlie would still shoot the otter, for catching
trout. That reminds me—I must examine that trout I brought
home last night."

.   .   .   .   .

" Just as I thought," said Mr. Thornley, peering through his
magnifying glass.

" What is it? " asked Robert.

For answer Mr. Thornley handed him the lens and pushed a little glass saucer across the table. Robert saw a mass of tiny creatures with big staring eyes, and bodies which seemed to have a round hump.

" Those are baby trout," said Mr. Thornley. " Those humps are the yolks of the eggs, still attached to their bodies."

" Baby trout? But the fish was a trout itself, wasn't it?"

" That's right—an old male. It isn't fussy about its food."

" What a funny thing," said Robert, " eating its own babies!"

" That otter was really doing the fishermen a good turn," said Mr. Thornley.

" Can't you tell them about it, sir?"

" I'll try. We must tell them about the heron too." He glanced at his watch. " Time I was off. You'll have to tuck me up in the hide this morning—the Keeper's busy."

They took the usual path through the woods, and as they approached the pheasant's nest Robert remembered the argument about the egg-thief.

" I say, Mr. Thornley, did you set that trap?"

" I did—and you can find it. Lead on."

He dropped back and let Robert go first. Robert walked slowly forward, searching for the thick honeysuckle. He passed two which didn't look right, but the third looked familiar, so he turned off to the left. Yes, there was the silver birch. He stopped by the birch, faced the oak, and began to count his steps, but when he reached ten there was no sign of the nest.

" Carry on," whispered Mr. Thornley behind him, " your steps are shorter than Jim's."

Four more steps, and suddenly Robert spotted the pheasant, crouching as still as a stone. The moment she was seen she rose like a rocket, making Robert jump. Mr. Thornley stepped forward, and bending down, picked up a wire cage-trap from behind the nest. Crouching inside it was a rat, with a long tail and bright beady eyes.

" Ah—another thief caught," said Mr. Thornley. " I'll leave it for Jim to deal with," and he put it down again.

" How on earth did you know it was a rat? " asked Robert.

Mr. Thornley grinned.

" I took a chance, I'll admit. You see, if a badger robs a nest—which does happen sometimes—he usually takes the lot. As for a hedgehog, it's my belief that in springtime he has plenty of beetles, slugs, snails, and insects to eat, without bothering to look for nests."

" Was that all? "

" No, not quite. When I looked closely on the ground I found a rat's droppings. You don't have to be fussy if you're a good nature detective."

" That's one in the eye for Jim, isn't it? " said Robert, with a grin.

" Yes—Jim doesn't like to admit he's wrong. He was brought

up to call badgers and hedgehogs vermin, so he shoots them on sigh
Never thinks of looking for evidence."

" I've never seen a badger," said Robert.

Mr. Thornley grinned mysteriously.

" You will—before you're much older," he said quietly.   Robe:
knew that tone, and he looked up eagerly.

" I went into Bob Blake's shop for some tobacco this mornin;
and he told me where there's a sett," said Mr. Thornley.

" What's that? "

" A sett—it's a badger's burrow.   There may be cubs.   It's in a
old sand-pit on the other side of the wood.   We'd better go tonigh
Jim will shoot them if he finds out about it."

     ·   ·   ·   ·   ·

Birds were singing all around as the two nature detectives settle
down to watch for badgers.   The sett was at the foot of an old sand
pit, and the watchers were sitting among the bushes at the top of th
bank.   Mr. Thornley had explained to Robert that in this situatio:
a hide was not necessary, as it was most unlikely that the badger
would look up.   What did matter was the direction of the wind
which luckily was blowing their scent away from the sand-pit.

For a long time nothing happened but the movements of birds
Robert watched a blackbird and a robin sing their good-night song
and fly off to roost.   He was beginning to get tired and let his min
wander, when he noticed a movement down below.   A badger
No, a rabbit.   Surely it had come out of the badger's burrow
It sat up on its hind legs, looked all round, and hopped away int
the shadows.   Robert watched closely, and to his surprise anothe
rabbit emerged from the burrow.   He turned to Mr. Thornley t

k him if he had mistaken the hole, when a loud " thump, thump "
)unded somewhere underground. " Thump, thump "—the sound
ime again—then a distinct grunt, like a pig. As Robert stared, he
.w a small grey creature creep out of the burrow. It seemed to
ave a white face. Surely a badger was bigger than that! The
ext moment his question was answered, for a much larger animal
raddled out and pounced on the small one. It lifted the small one,
wung it round, and dropped it in the mouth of the burrow. The
nall one gave a yelp, but the big one pushed with its nose and sent
ie small one headlong down the burrow.

The big badger paused and looked carefully about. Then it
fted its nose and sniffed. Robert could see its white face plainly,
nd the black stripes running along each side of it. As Robert
ratched, another big grey shape appeared. The two badgers
)uched noses, and stood looking round. One began to scratch
self like a dog, and the other trotted noisily across the sand-pit to a
ig pine tree, where it reared up on its hind legs and began to scratch
ie bark. Presently the first one joined it. It was getting dark,

but Robert could just see them, stretching their front paws upward like a couple of cats.

After a minute one badger wandered off to the right, and the other came back towards the two watchers. Robert could hear the sound of scratching and munching. He could just make out the white stripes on the face as the badger moved about in the shadows. It sounded as though it were eating something—surely it couldn't be pheasant's eggs? Shuffle, shuffle—the noise went on and on. It grew darker and darker, and then Robert did a dreadful thing for a detective—he dozed.

It seemed as if a long time had passed when he was woken by terrific bang. He jumped violently and clutched Mr. Thornley.

" Oh—what's that? " he cried.

" A gun," said Mr. Thornley grimly. " Listen."

Footsteps sounded among the trees over on the right.

Mr. Thornley stood up.

" Is that you, Jim? " he shouted.

" Aye, that's me," came the Keeper's voice.

" What have you shot? "

" An old brock. I'll bet he's the one who's been taking my eggs."

Robert felt a wave of anger rush over him. The Keeper had shot the badger, the shy mysterious creature that he had been watching only a few minutes ago. Mr. Thornley gave a sigh, and climbed over the fence to meet the Keeper, who was walking towards them carrying the dead badger by the tail.

" Got cubs, haven't they? " said the Keeper. " I'll dig them out in a day or two and finish them off."

Robert was horrified. He looked at Mr. Thornley to see what he

ould do. Mr. Thornley was looking very grim, but when he
poke his voice was quiet.

" Look here, Jim, what evidence have you got to prove that
adgers harm your pheasants? "

" Why, brocks are vermin, aren't they? " said the Keeper in a
one of surprise.

" That's just a name, Jim, and doesn't prove a thing."

" But everyone knows that badgers eat eggs," said the Keeper.

" Very well, we'll examine this one's stomach. No doubt we'll
nd it full of eggs. Then you'll be satisfied."

" Now look here, sir—he hasn't had time to eat many this
vening."

" Never mind, we'll see what he *has* been eating. We'll take him
ack to your cottage and examine him right away. Come on."

Mr. Thornley sounded so angry that the Keeper did not say
nother word. Nobody spoke as they walked back to the cottage
single file. Robert didn't enjoy the walk a bit, for the dead
adger was swinging in front of him all the way. He was glad to
it down by the fire, while the two men took the animal out to the
Keeper's shed.

The Keeper's wife tried to get Robert to talk, but he didn't feel
ke talking. He kept wondering what was happening out in the
hed. Presently the latch clicked, and the men came in.

"Well," said Mr. Thornley, " perhaps you'll take a bit more
otice of what I say next time."

The Keeper scratched his head.

" Bit of a surprise, I'll admit," he replied, " but you still can't
rove that they don't take eggs and birds sometimes."

41

" If you take your young pheasants straight from the coops an
put them on the ground in a wood, it's asking too much. You coul
easily wait till they're big enough to roost in trees, or you coul
train them to perch before they are put out in the wood. They'
be safe then. As for eggs—badgers take them sometimes, but the
don't make a habit of it."

A sharp knock sounded at the door, and the Keeper's wif
hurried to answer it.

" Good evening, Captain—won't you come in, sir? " she saic
Robert looked up and saw a smart, broad-shouldered man.

" Good evening, Jim," said the man as he entered. " Just com
over for a word with you about the birds. Hallo, Thornley—didn
know you were here. Anything wrong? "

" Jim and I have been having an argument about badgers,
answered Mr. Thornley.

" An argument? "

" Well, you see, sir," said Jim, " I shot an old boar badger thi
evening, and Mr. Thornley, he thinks I shouldn't have done."

" Oh! Well, why did you? "

" Well, sir, badgers is vermin."

" I see. Did you examine its stomach? "
Nobody spoke.

" Come on, man—speak up! "

" Yes, sir," said Jim, looking at his boots.

" What did you find? "
Jim glanced sideways at Mr. Thornley. " You tell him, sir."

" Very well," said Mr. Thornley. " We found the remains o
bluebell bulbs, worms, beetles, grubs, snails, and a young rabbit."

The Captain frowned.

" Tell me, Thornley, is this a badger's usual diet? "

" Yes, that's about it, with an occasional wasps' nest and a snake or two. They eat fruit in the autumn and they do sometimes eat eggs and even birds—but not very often."

" I see! Well, I like to have badgers about the place, so long as they won't ruin the shooting. I'm hanged if I want all the wild animals killed off just so that I can shoot a few more birds. We've spoilt the country enough already without killing off everything except pheasants. Just leave the badgers alone, Jim—you understand! "

" Very good, sir," mumbled the Keeper.

Robert let out such a loud sigh of relief that the Captain turned.

" Hallo," he exclaimed, " who's this? "

" He's my assistant—son of an old school friend," said Mr. Thornley with a smile.

" I see—and why are you looking so pleased, young man? "

" It's about the badgers, sir—I heard the Keeper say he was going to finish off the mother and cubs."

" Well, that operation's cancelled, so you'll be able to watch them another night."

" Thank you, sir. We were having a lovely time watching them."

" You didn't tell him you'd been asleep for half an hour, did you?" chuckled Mr. Thornley, as the Keeper's wife was saying goodnight to the Captain.

D

CHAPTER V

NOT GUILTY

" Going to be another fine day, sir," said Tom Wickenden, as he carried in a tray with eggs and bacon for two.

" Hope so, Tom.   How can you tell? " replied Mr. Thornley.

" That flock of crows—it's flying high."   Tom pointed out of the window.

" Tom, when will you get it right?   It's rooks that fly in flocks, not crows."

" Is it, sir?   I'm hanged if I can remember which is which."

" I know which is which," remarked Robert.   " We learnt a rhyme at school :

> Everyone looks
> At a flock of rooks,
> But nobody knows
> Of a flock of crows."

" There you are, Tom," said Mr. Thornley.   " Go back to school." Tom chuckled.

" Well, rooks or crows, they're all a darned nuisance—stealing corn and eggs, and picking up young birds."

Robert and Mr. Thornley exchanged glances.

" Another case for the nature detectives," said Mr. Thornley quietly.

" What's that? " inquired Tom.

" It just means that you've challenged us to prove that it's only rows which are harmful," said Mr. Thornley.

" How can you do that, sir? "

" You'll see."

After breakfast the nature detectives retired to their room to make plans.

" Now look, Robert, I've got a hide fixed up close to a kestrel's nest. I fixed it up two weeks ago, and I noticed a flock of rooks in the field beside it. The farmer had been sowing spring wheat. We'll go up there now, and we'll watch the rooks and the kestrels as well."

.   .   .   .   .

Robert was thrilled when he saw the hide, for it was high up in a pine tree. He could see a large nest of sticks in another pine tree close by. He wondered how they would reach the hide, but as they got nearer he noticed a rope-ladder dangling beside the trunk. Mr. Thornley was carrying his camera and some lunch in his haversack, while a boy from the farm had come with them, to leave the hide after they were inside. This was the real thing.

" Are the rooks still about? " Mr Thornley asked the boy, as they mounted the slope.

" Yes, sir, they keep coming. Dad shot one the other day, but it doesn't seem to make any difference."

" What have you done with it? "

" There it is, sir."

The boy pointed to a black shape dangling from a stick, which had been stuck into the soil in a corner of the field.

" Ask your Dad if I can borrow it for a day or two, will you? "

" That's all right, sir, you can have it," said the boy, as if he were giving a sweet to a little child.

" Mr. Thornley, what do you want the rook for? " asked Robert, as Mr. Thornley finished adjusting his camera.

" Now, Robert, you should know one reason. What did we do with the trout and the badger? "

" Oh, I know—we found out what they'd been eating."

" Quite right."

" What's the other reason, Mr. Thornley? "

" Ah—that would be telling."

They sat quiet for several minutes, while the breeze made the tree sway. This is how a bird must feel, thought Robert. He could look out across miles of meadows and woodlands, right away to the line of the Downs in the distance. It was a grand feeling.

Presently Robert noticed a bird circling above Forge Wood. He wondered if it were a rook—no, it couldn't be, because rooks fly in flocks. Could it be a crow? Suddenly the bird stopped moving. It stood quite still in the air, and Robert stared in surprise. Then it began to circle again. It swept out over the cornfield and stopped again, with its wings just quivering.

" That's the kestrel," whispered Mr. Thornley.

The bird circled again, and again it hung in the air on quivering wings—just like a spider on a web, thought Robert. Then to his surprise it raised its wings straight up and dropped. Down it went like a stone, spreading its wings again just as it touched the ground. Robert saw its head jerk downwards, and in a flash it was airborne again. It flew rapidly up towards the watchers, circled right round the clump of pines, and settled beside the nest.

The nest had looked empty at first, but now to Robert's surprise he saw a bird on it. It had a reddish-brown back and long pointed wings. It stood up as its mate sidled along the branch, and the two birds touched beaks. They stood side by side for a minute, staring boldly round with their bright yellow eyes, and it seemed to Robert that the one on the nest was slightly larger than the other. Very soon the smaller bird dived into the wind and flew rapidly away, while the other one crouched down in the nest.

" I didn't know that bird was there," whispered Robert.

" She came back when you were looking the other way."

" Is she bigger than her mate? "

" Yes, most birds of prey are."

" I say—what did he give her? "

" I expect it was a beetle."

" A beetle? "

" Yes, they eat lots of beetles, besides rats and mice and voles."

" Do they kill birds? "

" Not often."

" How do you know? "

" It's easy to tell what hawks and owls eat."

" You mean by examining their stomachs? "

" Oh no, a much easier way.   I'll show you later.   Keep quiet—I think the rooks are coming."

Down came the rooks, like a straggling army of black soldiers. They settled on the cornfield, and stood looking anxiously about, as if expecting danger.   After a minute they began to walk about and dig their beaks into the ground.   Robert smiled at the way they walked—they seemed to waddle like stiff-legged men, and the feathers which grew on the top part of the leg hung down like ragged black trousers.   Sometimes a rook hopped two or three times, as though it had seen something tasty and wanted to reach it quickly.   Robert wondered what they were eating.

" How can you tell them from crows? " whispered Mr. Thornley.

Robert looked closely at the nearest birds.   Something was different about the beak—it was longer and thinner—and surely crows didn't have that white mark where the beak joined the feathers.

" That white mark on its face," whispered Robert.

Mr. Thornley nodded.

At that moment there was a swish of wings and the kestrel alighted on its perch. This time Robert could see what it carried—a mouse-like creature with a short tail.

As the hen rose up with raised wings to receive her gift, Mr. Thornley took a photograph. Robert watched her hold the prize with one talon while she tore off a piece and swallowed it. She finished off the rest in one gulp and settled down on her eggs again while her mate flew away towards the wood. Robert watched the hawk hover three times, and then saw him drop behind a haystack.

" Was that a mouse? " he whispered.

" No—a vole. Didn't you see its short tail? It has a blunter nose than a mouse, and shorter ears. Watch the hawk—he's hovering again."

Back he came, this time with a rat, which both birds shared. The sight of the cock bird gulping away with the rat's tail hanging from his beak nearly made Robert burst out laughing.

When the kestrel had gone, Mr.

49

Thornley turned and pointed to a tall ash tree at the top of the corn-field. One rook was flying up to perch in the tree, and another glided down to join those who were feeding. Robert wondered why they were not all down together.

"That's the sentry-post," whispered Mr. Thornley. "One or two always sit up there to give the alarm in case of danger. Here, take the glasses and try to see what they're eating."

It was difficult to keep the glasses steady, for the hide swayed a little in the breeze. Robert could see the rooks poking here and there, and digging their long beaks into the soil, but there was no sign of any green blades of sprouting corn in their beaks. He searched the ground behind several birds as they moved forward, but the wheat did not appear to be eaten; only a few tiny plants were uprooted, and lay on the soil. As he watched, he heard a single sharp " Caw ". All the birds stopped feeding and raised their heads, standing like statues. The next moment the whole flock rose into the air, and flew away towards Forge Wood.

"What's happened?" whispered Robert.

"The sentry gave the alarm. Didn't you hear it? Look."

Mr. Thornley pointed towards the farm, and Robert saw a man walking slowly along behind a tall hedge. Through a gap in the hedge he noticed that the man carried a gun. The man reached the end of the hedge and began to walk towards them.

"Watch the kestrel," whispered Mr. Thornley.

The kestrel had flattened herself down until Robert could hardly see her. She was as still as a stuffed bird. Nearer and nearer came the man, looking left and right. As he reached the pines, Mr.

Thornley opened the flap at the back of the hide and called, " Cuckoo." The man looked up quickly.

" Hallo, sir—didn't know you were up there," he called.

At the instant he spoke, the kestrel slipped over the edge of the nest, and was away before the man had finished his sentence.

" I've got some pictures that will interest you, Jack," said Mr. Thornley. " I can show you this kestrel bringing voles and rats to the nest."

" What about the chicks I lost last week? See any of them? "

" We'll soon see if she's had them," replied Mr. Thornley, folding up his camera.

When they reached the ground Mr. Thornley picked up a number of small dry pellets and put them carefully into a paper bag.

" Rook-shooting again? " he asked the man.

" They were too quick for me this time, the rascals."

" Let's examine the ground where they were feeding," suggested Mr. Thornley.

They walked into the field, keeping their eyes on the soft soil. Here and there a bunch of sprouting grain was uprooted and lay on its side.

" Can't think why they pull it up and leave it," grumbled the farmer. He looked up to see Mr. Thornley walking across to where the dead bird hung on its stick. Mr. Thornley carried it back.

" I'll see if I can answer that question," he said.

Walking to the hedge, he slit the bird's crop with his pocket-knife, and emptied the contents on to a large flat stone. Robert was surprised to see a mass of little brown things like bits of string, and a few grains of wheat.

" Wireworms ! " said the farmer.   " By George—look at that ! "

" Let's count them," said Mr. Thornley.

The men counted in silence, while Robert looked on, wondering what it was all about.   Mr. Thornley finished first and stood up.

" Sixty-three I make it," said the farmer.

" I made it sixty-two," said Mr. Thornley, " but don't forget it would have been a lot more if you hadn't shot the bird."

The farmer was still staring at the stone.   " Sixty-three wireworms," he muttered to himself.

" Now you see why they pull up some of the plants.   Just think what that amounts to—say two hundred birds in a flock—that's roughly two hundred times sixty.   Come on, Robert, work it out—you went to school last."

" Six twos are twelve—and three noughts—that's—er—twelve thousand, isn't it? "

" That's right."

They walked back towards the farm without a word.   Robert kept glancing at the farmer, who looked very thoughtful.   As they approached an old tiled cart-shed, he pointed up to a little broken window in a loft.

" There's a white owl goes in there of a night.   The stairs are rotten, but you can fetch a ladder from the barn."

" Thanks.   Don't shoot her just yet, will you?—not till I can prove what she eats."

The farmer stood still, gazing up at the loft.   Then he slowly turned to Mr. Thornley.

" About the rooks—of course they do take corn in the stooks, but

52

I can always send someone up to scare them off." He paused, and gazed across the fields in silence. Then he went on :

" You know, you've reminded me of something my Grandad said to me when I was a boy. Fine old chap he was—what he didn't know about farming wasn't worth knowing. D'you know what he said?—'It's a poor farmer who can't keep a flock of rooks.' That's what he said. Well—good day to you."

He shook hands, and strode off towards the farm-house.

" What does all that mean? " asked Robert, as Mr. Thornley stood smiling at the farmer's retreating form.

" It means a victory for the nature detectives ! We've won him over to our side ! "

" Have we? He didn't say so."

" Robert, you town-people have got a lot to learn ! Why, he even showed us the owl's nest as a peace-offering. Come on—let's get that ladder."

When the ladder was ready Mr. Thornley told Robert to stand outside and watch the window. Robert heard a bump as the trap-door was pushed back, and at the same moment something which looked like a huge white moth glided out through the window. He had one glimpse of a white face with two large dark eyes. The thing startled him, coming so suddenly and silently. It flew away behind a barn, and he noticed its light brown back as it disappeared.

" Did you see it? " called Mr. Thornley.

" Yes—doesn't it look queer?   It frightened me a bit."

" You're not the first one.   Lots of folks have mistaken it for a ghost.   Here—come up and look at this."

Robert scrambled up the ladder and saw Mr. Thornley stooping in a dark corner.   Lying on the bare dusty boards were three round white eggs and a white fluffy ball.   When Mr. Thornley touched it it moved.

" Oh, it's got a face! " cried Robert.

" Yes, looks like a goblin, doesn't it?   Hurry up and help me collect these pellets.   We mustn't be long, or it will get cold."

   .   .   .   .   .

Back at the Fisherman's Rest the nature detectives were busy examining the pellets.   Mr. Thornley showed Robert how to dissect them with forceps, and separate little piles of bones, fur

54

and beetles' wing-cases. Mr. Thornley himself had the hardest task, for he had to decide which animals the bones had belonged to. Finally, every object had to be counted, and the results written in a notebook, with date and place of finding.

" Well, we know what these birds have been eating, anyway," said Mr. Thornley, looking up from his notebook. " See if you can remember, Robert. Let's have the kestrel first."

" Rats, mice, shrews, beetles—and those other little animals—what did you call them? "

" Voles—field voles. Which did the kestrel eat most of? "

" The voles. Then rats—then it was beetles, wasn't it? "

" That's right. What have you left out? "

" Oh, I know—a sparrow's skull."

" Right. Now give me the owl's menu."

" Rats, mice, voles, shrews—that's all, isn't it? "

" That's all. Any bones of chicks? "

" No. I say, Mr. Thornley—you haven't told me how the birds make these pellets yet."

" Sorry, I forgot. Well, you saw the kestrels gulp down their prey whole, didn't you? They can't digest fur and bones, or the hard parts of beetles, so these things form a pellet in the crop, and the bird just brings it up."

" About those rooks—don't they ever eat corn? " asked Robert.

" I'm afraid they do sometimes. We were lucky today. But they also do a lot of good, and they hardly ever steal eggs or kill little birds, as crows do. It's about time country people learnt which is which."

CHAPTER VI

CATCHING A ROBBER

"I say, Mr. Thornley—you said yesterday that there were two reasons why you wanted that dead rook. What was the second reason?"

Mr. Thornley looked up over the morning paper and grinned.

"I'll show you directly after breakfast."

Soon they were on their way to the Keeper's cottage. Mr. Thornley was carrying his camera and the dead rook. He spoke of a fox's earth, where he hoped to get some photographs of fox-cubs, but only smiled mysteriously when Robert asked him again about the rook.

When they arrived the Keeper was busy mixing food for his baby pheasants.

"Morning, Jim," said Mr. Thornley. "Is that old carrion crow still bothering you?"

"Ah, that it is. I've wasted hours waiting for it, but it always comes when my back's turned."

"You lend me your gun, and I'll see if I can get it."

The Keeper stared for several seconds without answering.

"You, sir? A gun, sir?"

"Bit unusual for a naturalist—but I want to try out an idea. I used to do quite a lot of shooting when I was a youngster."

"Very good, sir, you're welcome to the gun. You know where

t hangs. You'll find cartridges in the usual place. But you'll be a
sight cleverer than I am if you can get a shot at that old rascal."

"There's one more thing I'd like to borrow," said Mr. Thornley.
"That stuffed fox in your sitting-room."

The Keeper stared harder than ever. Suddenly he smiled.

"Very good, sir, you take whatever you want. There's no
telling what you'll be up to next."

He turned back to his work.

"You go out and look at the birds," said Mr. Thornley to Robert.
"I'll be with you in a minute."

Feeling very puzzled, Robert went out to the little meadow behind the cottage. Two large movable pens, like small chicken-runs,

stood close to the gate. The pens were roofed with wire netting and each pen contained six hen pheasants and one gorgeous cock They were kept for laying eggs, which were then set under hens.

Further off stood a number of hen-coops. Some had their fronts covered by a board, but Robert could see the hens in two of them, and near these two, little brown fluffy chicks were darting about. Robert walked nearer, and the chicks rushed to their coops to hide under their foster-mothers.

" Pretty, aren't they? " said Mr. Thornley, coming up behind him. He looked all wrong carrying a sack and a gun.

" Are they baby pheasants? "

" Yes, those are Jim's ' birds '. Just now they're treated like pet —but on the first of October the guns will be out after them."

" Seems silly, doesn't it? " said Robert.

" Don't you say that to Jim, or he'll think you're as crazy as I am Now let's see if my idea will work."

They went into the wood and followed a path which would take them round to the far side of the meadow without being seen. As Robert followed Mr. Thornley he noticed a queer object lying on the ground. It was brown and knobbly, and looked like some sort of cone with all the outside picked off. As he stopped to examine it, something hard struck the back of his neck. Robert looked quickly round, but could see nothing. He stared about in surprise Somebody was throwing things at him !

A faint rustle above his head made him look up. Something was moving high up on a pine tree, which stretched its branches across the path. Then he recognised the fluffy white tail-edges of a grey squirrel. It sat up on its haunches, holding something in it

ront paws, which it nibbled and turned. Brown scales came float-
ng down. As Robert stared, he heard Mr. Thornley's whisper:

" Now you know something else it eats."

" No, I don't—what is it? "

" Pine-cones. It eats the seeds."

Another cone dropped to earth, and the squirrel climbed out to the
ip of a swaying branch. Robert watched it nip off a cone with its
harp teeth and carry it back to a firmer perch.

" Time we were going," whispered Mr. Thornley.

They walked steadily along the narrow path, and twice they took
path to the left. Presently they stopped. Mr. Thornley looked
bout, and led the way through the trees till they reached the edge
of the wood. Robert could see the Keeper's cottage and the coops
on the far side of the meadow.

" Robert, can you slip through that fence without making a
ound? " whispered Mr. Thornley. " Right. Now take this
tuffed fox, and walk fifteen paces out into the field. Stand it up
acing to your right, and lay this dead rook just in front of its nose.
Then walk right across the meadow to the Keeper's cottage. Keep
out of sight if you want to watch."

Robert carried out his orders with great care and walked away
owards the cottage, wondering what on earth it was all about.
When he reached the cottage he went into the garden and lay down
behind a hole in the hedge. He could just see a dark speck which
was the stuffed fox.

He had waited for only about ten minutes when he heard the
harsh " Craw craw " of the crow. Tingling with excitement he
watched the small patch of meadow which was all he could see

through the hole. The cry rang out again, four times, and he caugh
a glimpse of a black speck swooping across in front of the distan
trees. Back it came, circling round—and then another spec
appeared. Straining his eyes, he thought he saw one land close t
the fox. In a few seconds the other speck glided down.

" Craw! craw! craw! " came the harsh note—then " Bang
bang! " Robert saw a puff of blue smoke against the distant trees
He almost jumped up in his excitement, but he remembered hi
orders and waited.

What was that? It was Mr. Thornley climbing through th
fence. Robert saw him stoop, walk a few steps, and stoop again
Then he stood up and waved. Robert rushed round to the gate and
dashed across the field. As he drew near, he saw Mr. Thornley pick
up the stuffed fox and start walking towards him.

" Did you get it? " panted Robert.

" I got the pair—look! "

" I say, Mr. Thornley—you must be a champion shot! "

" Used to be pretty good once, before I became a naturalist. I
comes in useful sometimes. There are criminals to be caught ever
in Nature. Take a look—Public Enemy Number One."

Robert turned one of the birds over in his hands. It was all black
from beak to claws. The beak was thick and strong, with a sligh
curve at the tip, and the nostrils were covered with stiff black
bristles.

" What a beak! " said Robert. " It reminds me of a dagger."

" It is a dagger. Many an egg and a young bird that beak ha
destroyed—to say nothing of mice, voles, and baby rabbits, or rab
bits caught in traps."

" How does it kill rabbits? "

" It's not very nice to admit, but it pecks their eyes. In hilly ountry it even kills lambs in the same way. Shepherds in the orth say that the crow is their worst enemy."

They looked up to see the Keeper's tall form approaching. Mr. Thornley held up the two crows.

" Here you are, Jim—I hope this will make up for our argument bout badgers the other night."

The Keeper stared as though he couldn't believe his eyes.

" Well, I don't know ! " he said. " Fancy you teaching me my ob. I have heard tell of that decoy trick, but I've never seen it done efore."

They walked back in silence. As Mr. Thornley handed back the un, the Keeper looked at him thoughtfully.

" You ought to have been a keeper yourself, sir. 'Tisn't many vho can claim a pair of crows with a right and left."

. . . . .

" Ever seen fox-cubs playing, Robert? " asked Mr. Thornley, as hey sat on a sunny bank eating their lunch.

" No, sir. I'd love to—I've only seen pictures of them. Do you hink we can? "

" We'll have a try. I know of a family in an earth in Furnace Wood, and the wind's right."

" The wind? "

" Yes, the wind—it's the most important thing to study when you re watching animals—more important than being hidden. It must low your scent away, or you're just wasting your time. We'll go ap there this afternoon."

" I thought foxes only came out at night."

" They do as a rule, but only because they have found it safer
Cubs often come out by day, until they learn that it's dangerous."

On their way to the earth Mr. Thornley stopped and pointed to
the ground.

" See anything, Detective? " he asked.

Robert looked very closely. Was it a faint track crossing the
path? The rushes on one side seemed to be bent and broken, and
on the other side the low brambles were parted. He looked more
closely, and noticed mud on the brambles where they were pressed
down.

" Go on, look closer. You're getting warm," said Mr. Thornley

Robert turned back to the rushes, and suddenly noticed the print
of an animal's foot in the damp soil.

" A track! What is it—a badger? "

" Oh no—you can't mistake a badger's track. It's much wider
and shows five toes. Try again."

" A cat."

" Not far out—but does a cat leave claw-marks? "

Robert bent down and noticed
four tiny dents close to the point of
the toes.

" Well, it must be a fox."

" It is. If you walk to those
bushes you'll get another clue."

When Robert reached the bushes
he bent down to examine the
ground and noticed a strong

peculiar smell.   Mr. Thornley chuckled at the sight of his wrinkled
nose.

" You've got it.   Take a good sniff and try to remember it."

" What is it? "

" It's the fox's way of letting others know that he has passed by.
He only makes it at special places, and that bush is one of them."

.   .   .   .   .

Robert was feeling drowsy, for the warm sunshine filled the little
hollow.   He seemed to have been staring at the two dark holes for
hours, seeing nothing but birds flitting about in the trees, and two
rabbits feeding.   Yes, rabbits—although this was supposed to be a
fox's earth.   He didn't dare to talk, but he wondered if Mr.
Thornley   were   mistaken.   Surely   foxes   killed   rabbits.   The
rabbits were all supposed to have been wiped out by that horrible
disease, but he had noticed quite a few about.   He began to watch
the birds.

Five more minutes passed, and Robert noticed something creeping
along behind some brambles.   It looked too big for a rabbit.   Then
a mischievous puppy-face came slowly up from behind the brambles,
a face with keen eyes and sharp pointed ears.   A fox-cub !

Robert was wide awake now.   He glanced at Mr. Thornley,
who was squinting through his view-finder.   The cub stretched up
to its full height, and the camera gave a tiny " click ".   Then the
cub pounced forward, right on to a second cub, which had been
hidden from view.   The two growled and snarled, till one broke
free and dashed across the hollow, hotly pursued by the other.   To
and fro they went, leaping over stones and brambles.   They went
right up on top of the bank and leapt down with a loud thump.

Then the fight broke off as suddenly as it had begun. One cu seized the dried-up wing of a bird, and carried it up to a sand mound under the bank, where it began to gnaw like a dog. Th other went into the brambles at the bottom of the hollow, an Robert could hear loud rustles, as if it were playing.

Mr. Thornley gave Robert a gentle nudge, and pointed to th brambles. Then he put his fingers to his lips and made a sucking noise which produced a shrill squeak. Silence. He squeaked again Suddenly there was a loud rustle and the cub in the brambles cam bounding out. It leapt on to a fallen tree and stood staring, ears up brush fluffed out, and whiskers quivering. Robert held his breath as Mr. Thornley took a rapid peep through the view-finder an pressed the bulb.

The cub started at the tiny click and crouched. Mr. Thornley made another squeak, but the cub was suspicious. It turned and jumped with a curious sideways spring, landing on a grassy patch In a flash it reached the entrance to the earth, where it paused fo another stare. Then with a whisk of its brush it vanished under-ground.

Robert let out a deep sigh.

" I say," he whispered, " wasn't that smashing ! "

Mr. Thornley nodded, and they waited for a long time, but there was no sign of the cubs. At last Mr. Thornley looked at his watch

" Twenty past four. We'd better be moving. I don't suppose they'll come out again before dusk."

Out in the sunshine they stretched their cramped limbs. Mr. Thornley walked softly to the earth, looking carefully at the ground. He picked up several bones and scraps of dried skin.

" What sort of evidence, sir? " asked Robert.

" Not too good, I'm afraid—a pheasant's wing, and bones of rabbits, and rats. This looks like a bit of rabbit skin—this must be a mouse's skin—and there's a mouse's tail. What's this? A frog's leg—and a hedgehog's skin turned inside out."

" It's a bit messy, isn't it? " said Robert.

" Yes, not like a badger's sett. Badgers are very clean; they even put their bedding out to air."

Robert grinned.

" That's right—I'm not teasing. I'll show you one day."

" I say, Mr. Thornley—you said rabbits' bones, didn't you? Well, how is it that there were some rabbits by the earth when we came? Aren't they afraid to come near? "

" It's a queer thing, Robert, but foxes don't usually kill game close to their earth. Those rabbits have burrows just under that tree. That reminds me—didn't you see some rabbits come out of the badgers' sett? "

" Yes, I remember. I meant to ask you about it."

" Rabbits often have burrows leading off from a badgers' sett. Perhaps the rabbits were there first. The badgers don't seem to interfere with them."

" People are always talking about foxes killing chickens and pheasants, aren't they? " said Robert, as they turned to go. " But don't they do any good? "

" Oh yes. Look at this evidence—rabbits, rats, and mice. And last March I received some evidence in the fox's favour from a most unexpected quarter—a Hunt terrier man."

" Who's he? " asked Robert.

" He's the man who is employed by the Hunt to carry a terrier with the hounds. It's carried in a box strapped to the horse' saddle. When a fox goes to earth, the terrier is put in after him The terrier makes such a noise that the fox often bolts, though he could quite easily fight the terrier."

" What happens if he doesn't bolt? "

" They dig him out and kill him. Nowadays they have to shoo him, but once they used to throw him to the hounds."

" I think it's cruel," exclaimed Robert.

" Yes, I'm afraid it is, but it's no use trying to convince the people who go hunting. They actually maintain that the fox enjoys being hunted."

Robert gave a whistle of disbelief.

" Now where was I? " said Mr. Thornley. " Oh yes, thi evidence. Well, the Hunt terrier man who wrote to me had examined the stomachs of all the foxes killed by the Hunt last season. There were twenty-seven altogether. How many do you think had been eating poultry? "

" I've no idea," said Robert.

" One. . . . The others had been eating frogs, rats, mice, hedgehogs, beetles, and slugs."

" I wish we could find some evidence like that," said Robert. " It seems a shame to kill them. They're such pretty things."

" Yes, and intelligent too—but I'm afraid that the ones who do take to killing poultry give them all a bad name. Hullo—what's this? "

He stopped sharply. Lying among the brambles was a dead cat. The leaves were trampled, showing signs of a fight.

" I say," said Robert.   " What killed it? "

Mr. Thornley stooped and examined the cat's claws.

" Look," he said.   He held up a tuft of reddish-brown hair.

" A fox? " said Robert in surprise.

Mr. Thornley nodded.

" Foxes often kill cats. I can tell by the way it's been done.
Now think—haven't you seen this old Tom before? "

" Oh yes, I remember.   It nearly caught a squirrel ! "

" That's it. It's a poaching cat. Vermin, Jim would say."

" Oh, then Jim would be glad it's been killed."

" I should say so ! A poaching cat does no end of damage to
game. I expect this one came too near the earth. We'll take it
along for evidence."

" I say, Mr. Thornley, perhaps Jim will kill the cubs if you tell him
about this earth."

" Oh no, he won't—not this time. I thought of that, and I
telephoned the Captain last night. He wants a few foxes for the
Hunt, so these cubs are safe anyway."

CHAPTER VII

UP WITH THE LARK

ROBERT was awake! There was a faint light in the room. A torch was shining, and someone was moving about. Was it burglars? He sat up sharply, and saw the shadowy form of Mr. Thornley tugging a thick pullover over his head.

" I say, Mr. Thornley—why are you getting up? "

Mr. Thornley turned round sharply.

" I thought you were asleep. You'd better lie down again—it's only ten past four."

" Where are you going? "

" I'm going to hear the Dawn Chorus and then watch the squirrels come out."

" Can I come? I'm not a bit sleepy. I shan't sleep any more now I know that you're going out."

Mr. Thornley paused a moment.

" Very well. You can come on one condition—that you lie down this afternoon. Put two pullovers on, and take your coat. It's always cold at dawn."

In a few minutes they were creeping down the stairs, by the light of Mr. Thornley's torch. Faint snores came from the landlord's bedroom, and the grandfather clock in the hall seemed to tick loudly enough to wake everyone in the house. They unbolted the back door and stepped out into the cold dark garden. As they hurried along the dim lane, everything looked strange. The river was covered with a thick cloud of white mist, which moved slowly along, and the shapes of trees stood up dark against the dull grey sky. Robert shivered.

"Feels queer, doesn't it?" said Mr. Thornley. "Never mind—you wait till the sun comes up."

He led the way swiftly through the shadowy wood till they reached the hide.

"Get inside," he whispered. "I'll put down some pigeons' eggs." Then he joined Robert, and pulled the flap into position behind him.

Robert was trying not to shiver, and was beginning to wish that he were back in his warm bed, when he heard a trickling sound, and realised that Mr. Thornley was pouring some liquid. A delicious smell of hot coffee filled the hide, and a steaming cup was pressed into his hands. As he sipped it, he decided that he had never enjoyed a drink so much in his life.

As soon as Mr. Thornley had drunk his own coffee he opened his notebook and sat ready with his pencil and his wrist watch.

"Going to note the first bird-songs," he whispered. "Have a doze. You won't see anything till it gets lighter."

Robert didn't mean to doze, but the hot coffee gave him a pleasant warm tingling feeling, and he was almost asleep when he was roused by a single clear bird-call. It sounded quite unearthly in the silence. He heard it again and again—very clear and shrill.

"Thrush," whispered Mr. Thornley, scribbling in his notebook.

Robert listened. The next bird to call was one he knew very well—a cuckoo. On and on it went, calling and calling. Then

came another song, softer and sweeter than the thrush. More and more birds joined in, and in a few minutes the air was full of bird-music. Mr. Thornley was glancing at his watch and scribbling as fast as he could, and Robert wondered how on earth he could recognise all these songs. He managed to pick out a skylark and a chaffinch among the babble of songs. He peeped out and saw that the second song he had heard was made by a fine cock blackbird. Then he saw a tiny wren fly to a stump and burst into a loud shrill song. The little bird trembled and shook its wings with the effort, and no wonder, for its song was as loud as any.

The full chorus went on for about ten minutes, and then began to die down. Robert noticed the light growing brighter. Then he saw something fly across the clearing and vanish into a hollow tree. It didn't look like a bird.

" A bat. A long-eared, I think," whispered Mr. Thornley. " We'll catch it later."

Robert tried to keep awake, but he felt drowsy. He leaned against the corner-post of the hide and dozed. He must have dropped right off to sleep, because when he woke up it was quite light, and he could see sunshine in the tree-tops. As he rubbed his cramped arm, he peeped out and saw the funniest sight—a squirrel yawning. She yawned three times, opening her mouth very wide. Then she stretched like a cat, front feet first. She shook herself, fluffing out her fur, and stamped her little forefeet on the branch.

After this she sat up and washed her face with her forepaws, going right over her ears, and then twisted round and gave her tail a thorough cleaning. When all this was over, she ran down the usual branch to the ground, taking exactly the same route as she had done before. She nosed about among the leaves, searching for maize, and taking no notice of the eggs. Very soon she climbed up the oak tree, and after nibbling a few buds and catkins, she sprang across to a beech tree, where she stayed in one spot for a long time. Mr. Thornley watched her through his glasses.

" What's she doing? " whispered Robert.

" She's eating beech bark. That's not so good. They often kill a branch by eating off the bark all round it."

Robert heard a rustle on the other side of the hide and saw the other squirrel racing along the swaying branches. It climbed right overhead. There was a sharp clatter of wings, and the pigeon flew off.

" Now we'll see," whispered Mr. Thornley.

Peering through a hole in the roof, the watchers saw the squirrel pass within a few feet of the pigeon's nest. It went straight on till it reached its mate, and the pair settled down to a meal of juicy beech bark. Mr. Thornley gave a sigh of relief and grinned.

" That lets him out," he whispered.

When Robert looked out in front again he noticed a pair of little black-and-white birds with long tails.

They kept calling to each other and

71

flying to an ivy-covered tree-trunk. Was that a nest, sticking out from the ivy, or was it just a bulge in the tree? He nudged Mr. Thornley and pointed. Mr. Thornley peered through the glasses, and handed them to Robert.

" A long-tailed tit's nest. I didn't know it was there. Something's upset them. Hallo—look ! ".

A grey squirrel was coming down the tree head first, with its tail fluffed out. It came down in jerks, looking sharply about, and seemed to be watching the birds. In a few moments it reached the nest. In went its nose and down floated bits of moss and feathers. Robert started to his feet, but a strong hand gripped his arm.

Suddenly there was a violent scuffle, and the air was full of harsh chattering cries. Two squirrels fell to earth with a thump, and scuffled there for a few seconds. Then one rushed off at top speed, while the other stood quivering all over, jerking its tail, and making its queer barking and whining cry. Gradually it became calmer and made its way up a tree, though its cries still sounded.

" What happened? " whispered Robert.

Mr. Thornley pointed up into the beech tree, and Robert was surprised to see that one of the squirrels was still there. He was completely puzzled.

" That one who robbed the nest was a stranger," whispered Mr. Thornley. " She chased him off because he was too close to her drey."

Robert was puzzling over this strange behaviour when he heard a sharp tapping. It sounded exactly like a visitor tapping on the door. Then he noticed a movement on the top of a sawn-off tree-stump. It was a bird with a bluish-grey back and a black eye-stripe.

" That's a nuthatch," thought Robert.

The bird began pecking with all its force, using its whole body. Presently it appeared to swallow something, and flew up into a tree.

" Quick ! quick ! quick ! " it called in a loud clear voice.

" What was it doing ? " whispered Robert, but Mr. Thornley was watching something.

A rabbit was hopping across the clearing, and there was something strange about its appearance. It seemed to creep along with its ears and tail down. Robert remembered that rabbits usually hold their ears erect and show the white fur beneath their tails when they hop. This one looked scared. Perhaps something is after it, thought Robert.

The rabbit had just crossed the clearing when the leaves rustled and another animal appeared, a long thin snaky creature, bounding along with a rippling movement. Robert had just had time to notice that it had a black tip to its tail when he heard a swish in the air, and an enormous bird swooped down. He caught a glimpse of a fierce hooked beak striking savage blows, while the animal writhed and hissed. For a second the bird stood still, staring about

with a defiant gaze, then the huge wings opened and it flew heavily away, carrying the dead animal in its talons. Mr. Thornley rushed out of the hide and stared upwards, followed by Robert. The bird soared above the tree-tops, circled round once with wings hardly moving, and then glided rapidly away.

" I say—was that an eagle? " asked Robert in a hushed voice.

" Next thing to it, son—it was a buzzard. I thought I saw one over Furnace Wood last week. It may have a nest somewhere near."

" Is it vermin? "

" Well, as it caught a stoat you could hardly call it vermin. I wonder if Jim will believe me. You see, stoats are one of Jim's worst enemies, because they eat his young pheasants."

" Do you think he'll shoot it? "

" He might. Most keepers shoot anything with a hooked beak and talons. A buzzard's usual food is rabbits, mice, voles, and even beetles, the same as a kestrel's. I think it made a mistake that time— it was probably after the rabbit. Never mind, it's evidence."

" What was the nuthatch doing? " asked Robert.

" Cracking a nut, I expect. They wedge them into the cracks in old stumps. Lots of the tapping which people think is made by woodpeckers is really the work of nuthatches and great tits. Didn't you think that mud door was a good idea? "

" Yes—but I'm sorry about the long-tailed tit's nest. It spoils our case for the squirrels, doesn't it? "

" Now look, son—get rid of the idea that wild creatures all act in the same way. A detective must accept all the evidence, good and bad. What we saw this morning proves that some squirrels take eggs and some don't—like boys. We've got to do a lot more work on squirrels before we can be sure about the amount of egg-stealing which they do."

" I see. Dad would say : ' the prosecution requires more time to collect further evidence '."

They hurried down to the main path. Dewdrops were sparkling on every bush, and birds were still singing. Just as they reached the path, Robert saw a tiny brown bird fly out from an ivy-covered trunk. When he peeped through the ivy-leaves he noticed a neat round hole, and found it was the entrance to a nest. The nest was made of dry grass and moss, and looked just like part of the stump.

Robert poked his finger in, but there were no eggs. Mr. Thornley had a curious twinkle in his eye.

" Any feathers inside? " he inquired.

" It doesn't feel like feathers. You try."

Mr. Thornley gently poked his finger in.

" No, I thought not. It's a cock-nest," he said.

" What do you mean? "

" It's another of Nature's unsolved mysteries. The bird you saw was a wren, and the real nest is built by the hen and lined with feathers. The cock bird usually builds several extra nests, but he doesn't bother with the feather lining. Sometimes he flies in or out of one of his nests right in front of you—as this one did."

" Why? "

" That's the mystery. There are all sorts of theories, but we can't prove a thing. Wrens often roost in their old nests on cold winter nights, and my guess is that these extra nests are built for roosting. This is a problem for you to start on when you become a naturalist."

" O.K. I'll make a note of it," said Robert.

F

CHAPTER VIII

HELD FOR QUESTIONING

AFTER breakfast Mr. Thornley went to his room to do some writing
Robert wondered what he should do, for to tell the truth he fel
rather sleepy. As he stood staring out of the window, the landlord
noticed him.

" Nothing to do, son? " he inquired.

" Well—I haven't decided yet," replied Robert.

" The rod's there if you want it."

" Oh, thanks."

" I should go out across the meadow this morning," said Tom
" See that big old willow over there? There's a nice shady poo
just below it. The light's a bit too bright in the open this morning.'

" I see. What bait shall I use? "

" You come with me. I'll show you."

Tom led the way to the garden-shed, where he picked up a fork
and a little tin. As they walked down the garden he looked sadly
at the neat rows of tiny lettuces.

" Just look what they mischievous slugs have done to them,"
he grumbled. " I keep putting stuff down, but the place must be
full of 'em."

At the bottom of the garden was a manure-heap. Tom stuck his
fork in and began turning over the manure. Presently he picked up
a tiny red worm.

" There—that's what you want for trout," he said. He put the worm in the tin. " You dig up half a dozen of them, and try your luck."

He walked back, giving another mournful look at his lettuces. Robert had just picked up worm number five and was turning over a fresh forkful of manure, when he saw the most astonishing sight. Buried in the manure lay a batch of round white eggs, about the size of a blackbird's egg. He stooped to touch them and found that the shells were soft. When he tried to pick one up, he discovered that the whole mass was stuck together. How could a bird hatch eggs which were buried in a manure-heap? He decided to cover them up again and ask Mr. Thornley at lunch.

It was very peaceful beside the water. Robert was so quiet that a moorhen swam quite close in its jerky fashion before seeing him, and a water vole came out of its hole in the opposite bank and sat on its haunches, eating the stalks of some tall plants which grew in the water. He could see its rounded nose and small ears, and wondered how people could mistake it for a rat.

Robert was nearly dozing when a splash made him look up. The vole was swimming under water and he could see it kicking out with its hind legs. It glided down and disappeared in some dark shadows. He was wondering how it stayed under so long when he heard a swish in the grass behind him, and saw Tom approaching.

" Any luck? " whispered Tom, sitting quietly beside him. Robert shook his head.

" Where did that old water-rat go? " whispered Tom.

" It went down there. It hasn't come up yet. How does it stay under so long? "

" It's got an under-water tunnel down there—leads up to its burrow."

" That's clever, isn't it? "

" Rats are a sight too clever.   Took most of my young chicks last year."

" But Mr. Thornley says those aren't rats—they're voles."

" Mr. Thornley's an educated gentleman and gives 'em all fancy names but any countryman knows that rats is rats! "

Robert sighed and gave it up.   Presently he caught one small trout, which Tom threw back, as it was below the permitted size. After that it was time for lunch.

Directly lunch was over Robert took Mr. Thornley down the garden and showed him the eggs in the manure heap.   Mr. Thornley smiled when Robert asked him what bird could have laid them.

" Look, Robert, these eggs are soft-shelled, and no normal bird

78

lays a soft-shelled egg. Can't you think of any other creature that lays eggs? Don't they teach you these things at school? "

Robert tried to remember his biology lessons. Yes, there was some creature which laid eggs.

" I know," he exclaimed, " it's reptiles—things like crocodiles ! "

" That's right. Can't you think of any British reptiles? "

" Lizards—lizards—oh and snakes ! "

" Right. These are snakes' eggs—a grass-snake's."

" Snakes are poisonous, aren't they? "

" Oh, Robert—what a remark from a nature detective ! "

Robert felt his ears going red.

" You go and lie down," said Mr. Thornley, " and I'll put up a net to catch that bat we saw this morning. I'll look out for a grass-snake too—I know a likely place for them. It's time I started a campaign on behalf of some of these little creatures. You can't argue with country people; you have to show them."

" Tom's like that, isn't he? He would have it that water voles are rats. He says they took his young chicks."

" Yes, I know. I've heard it all before. Now off you go, and mind you sleep."

Robert felt it was dreadfully babyish to be going to bed while the sun was shining outside. He put a book beside his bed, just in case he couldn't sleep. It really felt quite nice to lie down. He closed his eyes and imagined the river gliding past, smooth and cool, flowing on and on without a pause . . .

It seemed only a few minutes before the door creaked, and Robert woke with a start. Mr. Thornley was creeping in, carrying a small wooden box.

" I say—you have been quick," said Robert.

Mr. Thornley grinned.

" Not all that quick. It's gone four-thirty. I've had some luck this afternoon—look."

He raised the lid of the box and Robert found himself staring at the coils of a snake. He shrank back nervously. Mr. Thornley calmly reached into the box and picked the snake up. Its long smooth body hung limp, like a piece of rope. Then it raised its head and began to wriggle. Several times its head touched Mr. Thornley's hand, and Robert saw its little black tongue darting in and out. He felt scared, but he knew that it was silly to be afraid, because Mr. Thornley was so calm. Mr. Thornley grinned mischievously and held it right under Robert's nose.

" Like to hold it, Robert? "

" I—I—I don't think so—not just yet. Won't it sting? "

" Sting? It can't sting. Only insects can sting."

" Well, what's that little black thing poking out of its mouth? "

" That's its tongue. It's only a feeler. Look." Mr. Thornley held his fingers to the snake's nose, and the tiny black tongue flicked out and touched it.

" Well—how do snakes poison people? "

" With their fangs—special teeth which some of them have. This one hasn't any. I tell you what, Robert, we'll bring this snake out of his box after the Darts Match tonight, and show these men how silly they are to be afraid of it."

" That's a jolly good idea. Can't we do the same with the water vole? "

" We might—if we can catch one."

" Something's been eating Tom's lettuces. That wasn't a water vole, was it? "

" No, that was slugs. That's given me another idea—a hedgehog. Then there's the bat which I hope to catch tonight."

" Mr. Thornley, could we hold a sort of Court, and investigate all these charges? "

" That's just what we will do, Robert—if we can catch the suspects."

. . . . .

Mr. Thornley's exhibition of the grass-snake proved a great success. Men who started by being scared were coming forward to poke their finger-tips into its mouth, just to prove that its tiny teeth could not even prick them. They listened in silence while Mr. Thornley explained how grass-snakes can swallow frogs whole, and how they swim about in ponds searching for them. But when Mr.

Thornley mentioned water voles, Tom Wickenden began to argue.

"Look here, Mr. Thornley, this is all very well, but we've only got your word for it. I still think they're rats and they had my chicks."

"Well, Tom, there's only one way to prove it. We must catch one and find out what it eats."

"I've got a catch-alive trap I could lend you," said Walter Reeves.

"Yes, and I've got just the place to keep the creature in," said Bob Blake, who kept the village store. "It's a big water-tank, which stands in my back-yard. It's got soil and grass in the bottom. We could try out different foods, and see if this gentleman is right."

Everyone looked at Tom.

"I'm willing—and if it don't eat chicks and eggs I'll admit I'm wrong," said Tom.

At that moment a faint chinking sound was heard outside the back door. Tom looked up.

"That's old Tiddles—let him in, please, son," he said.

Robert moved to the door and opened it quietly. He saw a saucer gleaming in the dusk, but surely that little creature beside it wasn't a cat? As he stared, Mr. Thornley slipped past him. The creature darted into a flower-bed, but Mr. Thornley was after it in a flash. Robert saw him stoop and then spread his handkerchief on the ground.

"What on earth is it?" asked Robert.

Mr. Thornley did not answer, but poked something with his toe, and a prickly ball rolled on to the open handkerchief. He gathered up the four corners and picked up his captive.

"Just what we want," he said. "Now we'll prove what *he* eats."

"How on earth did you know it was there?" asked Robert.

"Well, I've noticed that on several nights, when that saucer chinked, Tiddles was sitting quietly on the window-sill. Look, he's there now. Hedgehogs are very fond of bread and milk."

He walked back into the inn and held up his handkerchief.

"Hey, Bob—have you got another tank?" he called.

The men crowded round as he laid the hedgehog on the floor.

"There's the chap who sucks my cows," muttered old Henry Martin.

"Don't talk daft, man," said William Turner, "that's just an old wives' tale."

A fierce argument started, and Robert was very glad to hear several men defend the hedgehog, saying that it ate slugs and snails.

"Let's have another test," suggested Bob Blake. "As it happens, I've got another tank. We'll try out this hedgehog with eggs— since some of you say he steals eggs."

"Best put one of Henry's cows in with un," interrupted George Goodsell.

The men laughed.

"Have you got any more creatures, sir, for this menagerie?" asked Tom, after the laughter had died down.

Mr. Thornley paused. He had a mysterious twinkle in his eye.

"Come on, sir—out with it," said Tom Wickenden. "You've got something up your sleeve, I'll be bound."

"As a matter of fact, there is another captive in my room at this moment," answered Mr. Thornley. "I caught him in order to try out a little experiment. I'll show you, if you would like to see it.'

" Go on, sir—we're willing."

" Right. Close all the windows—and bring in the ladies who are waiting in the tea-room, if they're not frightened. I shall also want some sticking-plaster, some scissors, and a ball of thick string."

The things were brought, while Mr. Thornley went up to his room and fetched another small wooden box. He showed the men how to tie strands of hop-string across the room from side to side, till they stretched in all directions. Five women entered and stood talking in excited whispers. Everyone stared at Mr. Thornley as he opened the box. He groped inside, and Robert heard a sharp shrill squeak. Out came Mr. Thornley's hand, grasping a bat, with immense ears as long as its head and body.

" Oooh," cried the women.

" Now, Robert—you'll have to be my assistant," said Mr. Thornley. Robert came forward, feeling very important, for all eyes were upon him.

" Cut a little piece of plaster about half an inch long, and don't touch the sticky side." Robert's hands were trembling a little with excitement, but he managed it.

" Now we're going to cover the bat's eyes with that plaster. I'll hold it steady, and you put the plaster on. Ready?"

It was a very tricky job, but Robert was lucky. The plaster went on smoothly.

" Good. That's excellent. Now, ladies, before I release this bat, would one of you volunteer to disprove the silly story that bats get tangled in ladies' hair?"

After some whispering, two women came forward.

" You're not frightened?" asked Mr. Thornley.

" What, frightened of that little mite —not me!" said one.

" Nor me!" said the other.

" Very sensible of you," said Mr. Thornley. He laid the bat right on top of the first woman's head, before she had time to protest. The bat raised its great ears and turned its head from side to side. Suddenly it vanished, and looking up, Robert saw it flying rapidly up and down the long room.

There was a dead silence. Up and down went the bat, never touching a wall, a beam, or a string. Robert could hear the faint rustle of its wings as it turned.

" You've played a trick on us, sir," muttered old Henry.

" No—no trick at all on my part," replied Mr. Thornley. " It's the bat who's playing the trick, and a very clever one too."

" But look here, sir, haven't you covered its eyes?" asked Tom in a puzzled tone.

" Oh yes, its eyes are quite useless at the moment."

" Well, look at it," protested Bob Blake. " It hasn't even touched a string. What's the secret?"

" I can't tell you for certain, but it's some sort of echo-location— something like radar. The bat keeps on squeaking, and it can tell what obstacles are in its way by the echo which comes back."

" Squeaking? I can't hear it squeaking."

" Oh no, we can't hear it. It's beyond the range of our ear but it's been recorded by instruments."

" Well, I call that wonderful," said Tom solemnly, and the me nodded.

Robert tugged Mr. Thornley's arm.

" I say," he whispered, " how are you going to catch it to get th plaster off? "

" You watch," said Mr. Thornley.

He climbed on to a chair by the window, and taking a fine string net from his pocket, pinned it to the top of the frame with drawing pins. Then he opened the top of the window. He had hardl left the chair before the bat darted straight into the net. Quick as flash Mr. Thornley was up on the chair, and the bat was in his hand opening its tiny jaws fiercely and trying to bite.

" Best let 'n go now," said Tom.

Mr. Thornley peeled off the tape and held up the bat.

" See its eyes? " he asked. " Yet people still say ' as blind as bat '. Queer, isn't it? "

He stretched his arm out of the window, and the bat vanished into the darkness. The men walked slowly back to the fire. A last the silence was broken by old Henry.

" Well, sir, I reckon we'll all take a bit of notice of you after that,' he said.

CHAPTER IX

ROBERT MEETS A GYPSY

WHEN Robert woke he saw that Mr. Thornley's bed was empty. He ran to the window, and there was the chief detective coming in through the garden gate with a thing like a wire cage in his hand.

" Any luck, sir? " cried Robert.

Mr. Thornley grinned and held up the trap. There was a small dark object huddled up at one end.

" I set it by his burrow late last night and he must have walked straight into it. Hurry up if you want to see him—he's scared."

Robert rushed downstairs and peeped at the trembling little water vole. It was quite different from a rat. Its ears were very small, and its nose was quite rounded, something like a guinea-pig's. Mr. Thornley covered the trap with a cloth, and as soon as Robert had dressed they hurried off to Bob Blake's shop.

In the yard behind the shop the nature detectives fitted up the two big tanks for their experiment. First of all they shovelled in a layer of soil, and after that Robert made a little den of bricks in the corner of each tank. He lined the dens with hay, and covered them with more soil. Mr. Thornley fetched pans of water and some big squares of turf, which Robert planted in the tanks. When all was ready, the hedgehog and the vole were each placed in a separate tank. The vole quickly disappeared into his den, but the hedgehog just lay where he was dropped.

" Thinks he's safe anywhere because he's got his armour," said M
Thornley. " That's why so many get run over at night. Whe
they hear a car coming they just curl up."

Bob Blake helped to provide the food for the test. The wate
vole was given several big bunches of water-plants, complete wit
roots, also two duck eggs, a bantam's egg, and a dead chick. Egg
were also placed in the hedgehog's tank.

" We shall have to wait till evening before we can find his prop
food," said Mr. Thornley.

" What's that, sir? " asked Bob Blake.

" Beetles, slugs, snails, mice, and sometimes adders."

" Adders, sir? They're the sort that stings, aren't they? "

" No, Bob, they don't sting, they bite. Adders have poiso
fangs, but hedgehogs kill them, all the same. If we could catch on
we could prove it."

" I'll tell the boys, sir, and we'll have a try."

. . . . .

At seven o'clock that evening Bob Blake's yard was crowded
and the Fisherman's Rest was empty. Every boy in the village ha
been out looking for slugs, snails, and beetles, and now the captive
were tipped into the hedgehog's tank, but it was a saucer of brea
and milk which aroused him. The men stood round in silence a
the little creature uncurled and gobbled up the food in the saucer
Then it scuttled rapidly round the tank eating the slugs and beetles
and presently the watchers heard the crunch of snail-shells.

" He ain't touched the eggs," whispered Bob Blake.

" That don't prove nothin'," growled Henry Martin. " You'v
given him so many slugs and small cattle that his belly's full by now.'

" We can soon settle that," said Mr. Thornley. " Give him
nothing but eggs tomorrow for the first hour or two."

" I wish he'd make his beat on my lettuce-bed," said Tom
Wickenden. " Did you see how he tackled the slugs? Swallowed
em down like oysters."

" Well, you can always encourage him with a saucer of bread and
milk."

" Couldn't you put some wire round your garden to keep him
in?" suggested Bob.

" It would take more than that to keep him in," said Mr.
Thornley. " Hedgehogs are good climbers—they can even climb
stone walls. It's a funny sight to see them get down again. They
just curl up in a ball and drop."

"What's the rat up to?" asked Henry Martin.

Mr. Thornley gave a sigh and looked across at Robert.

" The *vole* hasn't come out yet,"
he said, " and I
don't suppose he

will until we go away.   I suggest we look at him in the morning.

At that moment a step was heard, and the men turned to see the tall form of Jim the Keeper.

" Have you tried 'em on pheasants' eggs yet? " he asked.

" No—we didn't have any," answered Mr. Thornley.

" Perhaps these would do—they're clears."   He held out a small box.

" Thanks, Jim—I'll try them."

" What are they? " asked Robert.

" They're eggs that won't hatch," explained the Keeper.

" How do you know they won't hatch? "

" You hold them up to a strong light after they've been under the hen for a few days.   Those that are turning into chicks look dark but these look clear.   They're no use to me, so I thought Mr Thornley might as well have them for his experiments."

" I'm much obliged to you, Jim," said Mr. Thornley.   " If use pheasants' eggs I might convince even you."

The Keeper looked round to see if all the men had gone.   Then he took a step nearer and lowered his voice.

" Keep your eyes open, sir, when you're in the woods.   There's bigger vermin than hedgehogs about."

" What is it this time—fur or feather? "

" A two-legged 'un—and he don't fly neither."

Mr. Thornley raised his brows in surprise.

" Any suspicions? "

" Haven't got a clue, sir.   He knows his job all right.   I've found one of his snares today.   Mighty cunning affair.   Avenue snares call 'em."

" Why avenue? "

" Well, it's a little avenue of twigs stuck into the ground. Makes path about four inches wide. It's made right on my feeding-round, and baited with corn. A pheasant will walk right along etween the twigs, pecking the corn as it goes, until it comes to the nd."

" What happens then? "

" Why, then its head goes through a snare, but it don't see it, and : goes on moving forward until the snare pulls tight. The poacher ist comes along in the early hours and picks up his bird."

" Can't you wait up for him? "

" I have—for three nights—and I haven't seen a soul. Reckon e's lying low for a bit."

" Do you suspect anybody? "

" Only those Gypsies on Free Heath. Can't think of any village haps who are clever enough."

" Well, I'll certainly be on the lookout. Good night, Jim."

" I say, Mr. Thornley! " exclaimed Robert. " Isn't it exciting! . poacher! Do you think it is a Gypsy? "

Mr. Thornley shook his head. " It's the same old story, Robert— ondemning the prisoner without bothering to find the evidence."

" Do you think the Gypsies will get the blame for it? "

" Yes, I do. You can see that Jim has made up his mind already. le'll probably ask the Police to tell them to go."

Robert turned away, deep in thought. If the Gypsies were told ɔ go, he would lose the chance of meeting them. Besides, it wasn't ir. Why should they be blamed for something they hadn't done? le turned back to Mr. Thornley.

" Look here, sir—can't we try to find the real culprit?   You re
member the pheasants' eggs and the chickens."

Mr. Thornley nodded.

" Yes, Robert—that's just what we will do.   I'll finish writin
my notes this evening, and then we'll think of a plan.   Now I'
tell you what you can do while I'm writing.   You keep watch i
the hollow tree.   You may see the otters again, and you can also se
if any suspicious characters are about.   You're not afraid, are you?

" Afraid?   Of course I'm not," replied Robert indignantly.

" Off you go then.   Come back soon after nine and report t
me."

.   .   .   .   .

The evening mist was just beginning to creep across the river i
thin wisps as Robert settled himself in the hollow tree.   It was onl
ten past seven by his watch, and the sun had just set, so he had tw
hours.   Time to see the otter, if only it would show itself.   But th
water flowed with never a ripple, and nothing stirred but the littl
black moorhens, walking about like chickens in the far meadow.

After a long time Robert spotted the heron, gliding down som
distance upstream.   He saw it circle and lower its long legs, but ju
as it was about to land it rose again, and made off across the woo
Next moment the moorhens began to run swiftly towards the wate

" Something's scared them," thought Robert.

Suddenly he spotted somebody moving, creeping from tree t
tree, and paused for cover.   As the figure came nearer Robe
realised that it was a rough-looking boy, carrying a rod.   The bo
glided from tree to tree, bending low, till he reached a clump c
alders close to Robert's hide.   Here he stopped quite still fo

everal minutes, looking up and down the river. Satisfied that it was all clear, he baited his hook and cast out into the water.

For a long time nobody moved. Robert wondered who the trange boy could be, and what would happen if he were discovered. The boy looked rather big and rough. He might be Luke the Gypsy, but he might be the poacher! Robert decided that he had better slip away and report to Mr. Thornley. He peeped out on the other side of the tree.

He was just tensing his muscles for a dash across the meadow when he heard the swish of grass behind him, and turning swiftly he was horrified to see the mysterious boy running straight towards his tree. As he shrank back into a dark hollow a shadow blotted out the light, and heavy breathing sounded barely a yard away. Robert tood very still. He could see the back of the boy's head. What was he staring at? Then above the boy's shoulder Robert caught a glimpse of a man, moving slowly along the edge of the wood on the other side of the river. It must have been only a minute before the man disappeared, but Robert had never known time pass so slowly. He could hear his heart beating—" Thump! thump! thump! " Should he speak, or should he keep quiet?

Suddenly the boy turned his head. He gave a start and drew in his breath sharply. Robert tried to smile, but the boy's stare was ierce and suspicious, like that of a wild animal.

" What are you doing here? " demanded the boy.

" I—I—I only came to watch for otters," replied Robert in a rather shaky voice.

" You're spying for Keeper, aren't you? "

" No, I'm not! "

" You'll tell on me and spoil my sport."

Robert felt his face getting hot.

" I'm nothing to do with the Keeper ! " he answered.

" Aren't you one of his pals ? " asked the boy.

" No ! I don't like him ! "

" Oh ! " said the boy. " Why not ? "

" Well—he shoots things. He shot a badger we were watching the other night."

The boy looked interested.

" Who was with you ? " he demanded.

" Mr. Thornley. He's a naturalist."

There was a long pause.

" Does he take photos of birds and such like ? " asked the boy.

" Yes, that's right. He's jolly decent. He wouldn't shoot anything except crows."

The boy nodded mysteriously and said nothing. Robert noticed that the angry look had disappeared from his face.

" I say," he exclaimed, " do you know him ? "

The boy grinned. Robert was longing to ask him if he were a Gypsy, but somehow he didn't dare.

The boy turned and peeped out of the hollow tree. For several minutes he scanned the woods across the water. Then he turned back to Robert.

" It's all clear—he's gone," said the boy.

" Is he the poacher ? " asked Robert.

" Him ? No. He's the Keeper."

At that moment a loud splash sounded from the river, and both boys started. Two dark objects appeared in the water, gliding

swiftly upstream. The first one dived, followed by the second, and for a few moments there were only ripples to be seen. Then a black shape appeared on the river-bank. Was it an otter? Yes—Robert could see its blunt head plainly, and its thick tail. It galloped to a little mound and paused, turning its head from side to side. Another otter appeared, following the first, but just as it reached the mound, the first one lowered its head and slid straight down the steep bank into the water. Down went the second otter after it—Splash! Splash—then silence. The ripples glided away, and all was still once again.

The strange boy turned back to Robert. His dark eyes were shining, and he grinned with delight.

"I've never seen them slide before!" he exclaimed.

" Neither have I. I bet Mr. Thornley would like to have seen that ! "

There was an awkward pause.

" I say," said Robert. " I don't want to spoil your sport. I won't say anything about your fishing. Honest."

The boy stared hard.

" Is that a promise ? "

" Yes—on my honour." Robert held out his hand. Slowly the boy stretched out his own, and they shook.

" Right. You keep your promise and we'll be pals. Know anything about fishing ? "

" Not much, but I'd like to learn."

" I could teach you some tricks the anglers have never seen, but I mustn't show myself till after dark."

" Why not ? "

" I haven't got a permit to fish. The Keeper would have us moved on if he was to catch me."

" I say—are you a Gypsy ? " exclaimed Robert. The next moment he wished he had not spoken, for the suspicious look came back into the boy's eyes.

" Well—what if I am ? " he said angrily.

" I say—I've been wanting to meet you. Mr. Thornley told me all about you. He says your Dad is a friend of his, and he says you know lots of secrets about wild creatures. I should like to be friends with you too."

For several seconds the boy stared at him without speaking, and Robert was afraid that he had upset him.

" So you want to be pals," said the boy at last.

" Yes."

" What's your name? "

" Robert Armstrong."

" Mine's Luke Loveridge."

At that moment the sound of the church clock striking nine floated across the valley.

" Oh bother! " exclaimed Robert. " It's time for me to go. I promised to be in soon after nine."

Luke grinned.

" I'm glad I'm not a gorgio. The best part of the night is just beginning." An owl hooted as he spoke, and the mysterious call echoed among the trees. Robert sighed.

" I wish I could stop," he said.

" I stop out all night sometimes," said Luke.

Suddenly Robert had a brilliant idea.

" I say—I'll ask Mr. Thornley if I can camp out one night. He's got a tent."

" That's an idea. Come tomorrow. The weather's just right for fishing."

" All right. I'll meet you here tomorrow, and I'll bring the tent if he'll let me. I shall have to go now. I promised Mr. Thornley wouldn't be late."

" Well, so long, pal," said Luke. " See you tomorrow."

" Good night, Luke."

Robert hurried home across the fields, his mind full of exciting thoughts.

CHAPTER X

GYPSY SECRETS

Robert had an exciting tale to tell Mr. Thornley when he reached the Fisherman's Rest.

"I'm glad you've made friends with Luke," said Mr. Thornley. "It isn't easy to become friendly with a Gypsy. Tell me, did he use the word 'pal'?"

"Yes—I think he did, when we said goodbye."

"That's a good sign."

"Do you think I could camp by the river tomorrow night and do some fishing with him?" asked Robert, half expecting Mr. Thornley to say no.

"Well, I've camped with Gypsies many times, so I can hardly say no to you. All right—you can borrow my tent."

.   .   .   .   .

Next morning Robert hurried round to Bob Blake's yard with Mr. Thornley, and they peered into the tanks which housed their captives. In the vole's tank the eggs lay untouched, and the dead chick too. Only the plants had been eaten.

"Looks as though you're right about him, sir," said Bob Blake. "I'd better bury that chick."

"Don't bother. Just drop it into the other tank," said Mr. Thornley.

"Oh, so hedgehogs will eat them."

" Yes, if they can catch them—which isn't very often. No doubt they eat young ground-nesting birds at times. But when you think of the thousands of slugs, snails, caterpillars, and beetles which they eat. . . ."

" Yes, I see what you mean, sir. You might say that they take a fair wage."

" The next point to settle is whether hedgehogs eat eggs," said Mr. Thornley.

" Yes, sir. When the men come round this evening I'll try master hedgehog on eggs for the first hour, like you suggested."

. . . . .

At seven o'clock that evening Robert was carrying Mr. Thornley's light-weight tent towards the river. It was hard work, for a sleeping-bag and a ground-sheet were rolled up inside the tent, and Robert had to stop and rest several times. He kept wondering what tricks Luke would show him, and whether he would find any more clues about the mysterious poacher.

When he reached the tree, Robert looked about for a good camping site, and decided on the little knoll where the otter had appeared. As he unrolled the tent an envelope fell out. It was addressed to him. He tore it open, and found two fishing permits, bearing the names ' Robert Armstrong ' and ' Luke Loveridge '. Folded inside it was a note, which said :

Dear Robert—These may be useful if Jim comes to investigate. Don't be surprised if you have a visitor round about ten o'clock.

J. T.

" Jolly decent of him," said Robert to himself.

He started to put up the tent, and was bending over a guy-rope when he heard a low whistle, like that of a bird. Turning his head, he saw something move under the alders. He hurried across, and there stood Luke, leaning against a trunk, so that from a distance he was almost invisible.

" Can't come out yet," whispered Luke. " Keeper might nab me."

" It's all right—I've got permits for both of us," replied Robert, feeling very important.

Luke's eyes showed surprise.

" How did you manage that, pal? "

" Mr. Thornley fixed it—oh, and that reminds me—we want to find out who the poacher is."

" Have they got any suspicions? "

" Well, the Keeper did say that none of the village men were clever enough to think of the kind of snare he found."

" So he said it was Gypsies," said Luke.

" Yes, he did. How did you know? "

" They always do. What did John Thornley say? "

" He didn't agree. He said we'd have to start being real detectives, and find the culprit."

Luke grinned mysteriously.

" I say—I do believe you know who it is," exclaimed Robert.

" I've got a pretty good idea. We don't miss much that goes on after dark."

" Well, you tell the police, and then you won't get the blame for it."

Luke shook his head.

" 'Tisn't as easy as that. I've got no real proof—and anyway, who'd believe a Gypsy?"

" Isn't there anything we can do?"

" No, not unless he gives himself away. Let's start fishing. Which do you fancy, worms or dry-fly?"

" I've only tried worms," said Robert, feeling very ignorant.

" That's the best place for worms," said Luke, pointing to a muddy stretch where cattle had been drinking. " Here's a tin of little red ones, and a rod. I'll go down just below these trees and try the fly." He slouched off, leaving Robert feeling rather bewildered. Robert went to the spot, baited his hook, and cast out. He sat on the bank, and watched the gliding water, and Luke's still form, which looked rather like an old stump. He hoped very much that he would have the first bite, for he felt such a beginner.

Twilight began to creep across the valley, and a white owl

appeared, flying low above the hedgerows as it searched for its prey
Robert was watching it when out of the corner of his eye he noticed
his float moving. Holding his breath, he tried to judge the right
moment, and jerked back his rod. Yes—a bite—a silvery dancing
fish, scattering drops of shining water. Robert pounced on it
eagerly. As he knelt in the damp grass he glanced across at
Luke, and saw his rod swing back. He had just managed to beat
him.

Robert was trying to remove the hook without hurting the fish
when he heard the grass swish, and there stood Luke, with a broad
grin on his dark foreign-looking face.

" Jolly good, pal—I was watching you. You've got the right
idea." He stood grinning while Robert fumbled with the fish.

" I hate doing this," said Robert, feeling rather small.

" Pull it right through—it don't seem to hurt 'em," said Luke
" Like this." He went to take hold of the fish, but stopped. Away
downstream came the harsh cry of the heron. Luke looked at
Robert.

" Shall we see if we can catch him? " he asked.

" Catch whom? "

" Old Jack Heron—with this fish. Come on—I'll show you."

Snatching up the fish and the rod, Luke ran swiftly upstream
with Robert behind him. He reached a shallow stretch and walked
straight in. Holding the fish under water, he removed the hook
and told Robert to reel in. As Robert did so, he saw Luke stoop
and plunge both arms under water. After a minute Luke scrambled
out and ran back to the shelter of the trees.

" What did you do? " panted Robert.

" You'll see—if we catch him.   Let's get back on the job."

Robert watched the gliding water again and wondered what Luke had done.   The light was fading now, and the woods across the water looked black and mysterious.   Luke caught another fish, and presently he came creeping up to fetch Robert.   They moved quietly downstream to another spot, and here they caught two fair-sized trout.

" How do you know where to go? " whispered Robert.

" You watch the fish, and get to know where they feed and where they lie. . . ."

He broke off, for the harsh scream of the heron rang out, followed by the sound of splashing and flapping.   Without a second's pause, Luke was dashing upstream, and Robert was pounding along behind him.   When Robert reached him, Luke was standing in the shallow water.   Robert watched him take two careful steps and make a lightning grab.   Then came a mighty flapping and splashing.

" Come and hold his wings," cried Luke, as Robert slid down the bank.   Half blinded by the beating wings, he grasped them and hung on, until Luke secured them under his free arm.

" I daren't let go his beak," panted Luke.   " Here—feel this line? It's tied to a stone.   Cut it off short."

Robert cut the line, and they climbed up the bank, wet and triumphant.

" What shall we do with him? " asked Luke.

" I'd like to keep him until Mr. Thornley's seen him.   I say, how on earth did you catch him? "

" Quite simple.   You hook a live fish on to a good strong line, and tie the other end to a stone or a branch, so that the fish is in the water. If Jack Heron sees him he swallows him, and there he is—caught."

" What about the hook? Won't it hurt him? "

" Well, herons spit out pellets of fish-bones and fur, so I guess th hook comes up in one of them. Hey you—keep still! "

A loud owl's hoot sounded close at hand, and Luke started.

" Listen! That's no owl," he whispered.

The cry sounded again.

" I know—it's Mr. Thornley," said Robert. He tried to hoo back, making Luke smile.

In a few moments a tall form appeared out of the shadows.

" That you, Robert? " came a voice.

" Yes—look what we've got for you. A heron! "

" What luck, " exclaimed Mr. Thornley. " It's just what I want A friend of mine is doing research on herons. It's a good job brought this sack to sit on."

He held the sack open while Luke guided the sharp beak into the mouth. A quick jerk, and the bird was in. Mr. Thornley closed the mouth and tied it with a piece of string.

" Hope he'll be quiet for a bit—anyway till we've had our supper," said Mr. Thornley.

" Supper? " said Robert.

" Yes—I've brought Luke's favourite supper." He plunged his hand beneath his coat and pulled out a large warm parcel. There was no mistaking that smell.

" Fish and chips! " exclaimed Robert. " Oh yes—I remember the paper."

In a few minutes they were sitting beside the tent, eating fish and chips with their fingers. Robert thought food had never tasted so good.

" Well, what's the news? " asked Mr. Thornley.

" Oh, I forgot to tell you," said Robert. " Luke knows who the poacher is ! "

Mr. Thornley nodded calmly.

" I thought he would," he said, looking across at Luke with a smile.

Luke hesitated a moment, and then grinned shyly.

"We all know who it is," he said. " It's Joe Turner, the postman."

Mr. Thornley looked surprised.

" Good gracious ! The cunning rascal ! Nobody would suspect him—and your people are getting the blame for it. We must set a trap for him."

He thought for a minute in silence. Suddenly he leaned forward.

" I've got it ! Look here, Luke, can your people have all the poacher's snares watched, and send me word directly he catches a bird? "

Luke nodded.

" Give this message to your Dad." He scribbled something on a piece of paper and handed it to Luke. " Cheer up, Robert, I think this plan should work. Now I'll be off with the heron. Don't stay up too late. Good night."

Luke sat very still and silent after Mr. Thornley had gone, and Robert wondered what he was thinking.

" Do you think we shall catch the poacher? " he asked.

Luke nodded.

" He helped us once before, in the New Forest.   We haven't for
gotten it."

" Why do you always get the blame for poaching? "

" Well, we often catch a rabbit or a hare for the pot, but we neve
catch game to sell, like the gorgios."

" What does that word mean? "

" It means people who are not Gypsies."

" It doesn't sound a very nice word," said Robert, and Luke
smiled.

" Most gorgios aren't very nice to us.   We don't trust them.
I should never have come fishing with you if it hadn't been for
John Thornley."

" I hope you trust me," said Robert anxiously.

" Don't worry, we're pals now," replied Luke with a smile.

Robert felt honoured.   He could not think of anything to say, so
he wisely said nothing.   The boys sat in silence for a few minutes,
listening to the rippling water and the distant hooting of owls.

" It's lovely out here at night, isn't it? " said Robert after a long
pause.   Luke nodded.

" I'd hate to sleep in a house," he said.

" Haven't you ever slept in a house? " asked Robert in surprise.

" Not I.   We usually sleep out.   We only sleep inside the vardo
if it's very cold."

" Inside what? " asked Robert.

" Inside the vardo.   Haven't you ever seen a vardo? "

" Is that what we call a caravan? "

" Yes, that's it.   You must come and see ours in the morning."

" I'd love to," replied Robert.

Luke smiled and rose to his feet.

" I'll show you another way to catch fish," he said. " Got a torch on you? "

Robert felt his pocket. Yes, he had remembered to bring one. He nodded.

" Good," said Luke.

He led the way to the river, dropping to his hands and knees as he approached the bank. The boys crawled to the edge of the water and lay down in the damp grass, with the water gliding past just below their faces. Luke slipped his right hand gently into the water, and held it close to the bank. With his left hand he switched on the torch, and held it out so that it shone down on the water. The light was reflected back on to his face, and Robert was fascinated by the strangeness of the sight—just a face, surrounded by shadows.

A sudden movement in the water caught his eye, and he glanced down. Was it a fish? Yes, a big one. It glided downstream, turned with a lazy flick of its tail, and hung there motionless, staring up at the light. The next instant the smooth water was broken by a lightning sweep of Luke's right arm, and the fish shot into the air and landed on the bank. Robert had pounced on the wriggling creature before he realised what he was doing.

" Well done," whispered Luke in his ear. " Put it in the bag."

They lay down again, and Luke caught two more. Then the fish became nervous, so the boys moved a little way upstream. They lay down again, and Luke handed the torch to Robert.

" You try," he whispered.

Robert switched on the light and waited. He was tingling with excitement. He stared at the dark water sliding swiftly past until

he began to imagine that he was a fish himself. Perhaps the whole thing was a dream, and he would wake up in bed. What was that? Something flickered in the beam, and there was a fish, its big round mouth opening and closing. He made a swift grab with his right hand, but missed, and the fish vanished in the swirling water.

"Try again. Reach out a bit further," whispered Luke. "They always look nearer than they are."

Robert waited while the ripples died away. Yes, he should have remembered that things under water are never just where they appear to be. He remembered a lesson at school about refraction of light. How did it work? He was trying to recall the diagram in his notebook when the water swirled and an enormous fish appeared. It seemed to hang there, tail downwards, gaping at the torch as

hough it would swallow it. Robert took a deep breath, then
' Swish "—his right arm shot out. He felt the sharp impact of
omething heavy and saw the fish rise into the air. When he got to
his knees, Luke was sprawled full length in the grass behind him, and
here was something wriggling in his hands.

" Well done, pal—he's a beauty," exclaimed Luke. " He'll make
a lovely breakfast."

" What is it? "

" A trout. He's bigger than any I've caught."

They stood up, and Luke put his hand on Robert's shoulder.

" You're doing fine, pal. You're pretty smart for a gorgio."

" Thanks awfully," replied Robert. He felt so happy that he did
not know what to say. Suddenly he yawned, and Luke's quick
eyes noticed.

" We'd best be getting some sleep," he said, and led the way back
o the tent. As they passed a bush he bent down and pulled out a
rolled blanket.

" Are you coming in with me? " asked Robert, as they reached
he tent.

" I'd rather sleep out tonight. Tents get stuffy. Why don't you
sleep out with me? "

" All right," replied Robert. Nothing seemed impossible tonight, even sleeping in a field. He pulled out the ground-sheet and
sleeping-bag, and laid them on the grass. Then he took off his
shoes and his jacket, and wriggled into the sleeping-bag. Luke
gathered a pile of dry bracken, rolled up his jacket for a pillow, and
tucked the end of his blanket under his feet.

" Good night, pal," he said.

Robert lay awake for a time looking up at the stars, and listening to the rippling water. Now and then an owl hooted, and a wild duck quacked. He made up his mind to come again. He would like to sleep out every night, if only the ground were not so hard. At last he fell asleep, still wondering if he had imagined the whole adventure.

CHAPTER XI

AT HOME WITH THE GYPSIES

A HARSH cry woke Robert. He sat up, and saw a big grey heron flapping heavily past. He turned to speak to Luke, but Luke had rolled up his blanket and gone.

Robert began to rub his right arm, for it felt terribly stiff. The sun was rising above the wooded hill in front of him, and the wet grass sparkled with millions of dewdrops. Everything looked new and clean. He had never seen the sunshine so bright, or the sky so clear. How different from mornings in London.

A wood-pigeon began to call, and another answered it. Robert had just spotted the first bird when it flew from its tree-top and mounted up steeply into the air. He could see the sun shining on its blue-grey back and white wing-patches. Then the bird clapped its wings three times, spread them wide, and glided downwards.

"Lovely," thought Robert. "I wish I could do that."

A rustle in the grass made him turn and he caught sight of Luke, picking up sticks. Luke had lit a fire on the river-bank, and the clean white smoke was rising straight up into the air. Beyond it lay the smooth shining water, reflecting the green of the further bank.

"It's perfect," thought Robert.

Luke caught sight of him and waved. Robert slid out of his sleeping-bag, put on his shoes, and walked across to join Luke.

"Hallo, Luke. Isn't it a lovely morning?"

Luke turned and smiled.

" I thought you'd like it. Feel like a bit of food? "

" I didn't bring anything to eat," replied Robert. He looked down and was surprised to see a frying-pan, two tin plates, and a loaf.

" Where did they come from? " he asked.

" I hid them on a ledge in the old tree," replied Luke. From a rolled-up newspaper he unwrapped some cooking fat, and placed some in the pan. He set the pan across two large stones which stood in the fire. Then he unwrapped the big trout from between some large leaves and prepared it for the pan. Soon it was sizzling merrily.

" It smells lovely," said Robert.

When the fish was cooked Luke fried two large rounds of bread, and in a few minutes they were sitting on the edge of the bank enjoying their breakfast. As they finished, they heard the church clock strike seven.

" Have you been up long? " asked Robert.

" I'm always up pretty early."

" Did you see anything interesting? "

" I saw a vixen taking a rabbit up into Furnace Wood. She came over the bridge." He pointed to a rough wooden bridge several hundred yards upstream.

" Can't foxes swim? " asked Robert.

" They can, but they use bridges where they're handy. You can tell by their tracks when it snows. I saw lots of moorhens, some mallard, and a couple of herons. One woke you up, didn't it? "

" Yes, it did. Where have they all gone now? "

" They hide away during the day. Night time and early morning is when the game's about. How about coming to see the ardo? "

They wiped their plates and the pan with dry grass and soil, which to Robert's surprise cleaned them better than hot water. Luke stowed his things away inside the hollow tree and led the way upstream, after making sure that the fire was stamped out. They followed the river till they came to a lane, where they turned right, but they had not walked far along the lane before Luke stopped.

" Listen," he said.

Robert listened. Somewhere ahead he heard the rapid " clippety-clop " of a galloping horse.

" I bet that's the Captain's hunter," said Luke in a low voice. ' She's run away before."

They waited, while the sound came nearer. Luke glanced rapidly up and down the lane.

" It's narrow here. We'll catch her," he said.

" I don't know anything about horses," said Robert.

" Never mind. You just do what I do."

In another moment a tall chestnut mare appeared. Her gallop slowed to a canter as she spotted them. Luke began to walk slowly backwards, and Robert kept level with him. As the mare approached Robert noticed her wild-looking eyes and tossing mane. He didn't fancy this at all.

" Come on, girl—come on," called Luke, walking slowly back.

The mare was only ten yards away when she stopped and snorted. Then she began to walk slowly towards Luke, with her nose stretched out. When she was only a few feet away Luke stopped,

and the mare stopped too. She stretched out her nose until it wa
nearly touching his face. Then the wild look went out of her eye
and she lowered her head and allowed him to pat her.

" I'm going to ride her back," said Luke in a low voice. " It'
the first big house you come to, about half a mile ahead. Meet m
there." He twisted his fingers in the thick mane, gave a sudder
spring, and landed on her back. She was quiet now. Luk
turned her by patting her neck, and trotted away.

" I wonder how he did it," said Robert to himself.

He hurried along the lane, which cut right through Furnac
Wood, not far from the fox's earth. When he came out of th
trees he noticed a big house in the valley ahead. He ran down th
hill, turned in at the big iron gates, and followed the drive till h
came to the house. He noticed the stables standing to one side o
the house, and as he reached them he caught sight of Luke, talkin

with two men. They turned to glance at him, and he recognised one as the Captain.

" Well, young man—I understand you helped this lad to catch my mare," said the Captain.

" I didn't do anything, sir," panted Robert. " It was Luke. She was ever so wild, but he made her quiet."

" I wish my groom could do the same," grumbled the Captain. ' I'm very much obliged to you boys. Last time she got out she an for miles, and injured her leg. Tell me—what can I do for you n return?" He fixed his hard blue eyes on Robert, but Robert knew that the Captain was not so hard as he looked. He remembered the badgers.

" Please, sir, could you give us permission to walk through your woods?" he replied.

" Very well. Permission granted."

He turned to Luke.

" Are you camping on the Heath?"

" Yes, sir."

" What's your name, my lad?"

" Loveridge, sir."

" Ah. Had a Loveridge with me in Burma—wonderful chap at scouting—made rings round the Japs—came from Dorset. Any relation?"

" My Dad was in Burma, sir."

" Indeed. I must come and see him. Well—good morning."

He turned smartly and strode away to the house, followed by the groom.

" I say, do you think he really knows your Dad?" asked Robert.

" Maybe.   Dad doesn't talk much about the War, but I know h
was in Burma."

" How did you make the mare so quiet? " asked Robert, as the
walked down the drive.

" It's an old trick.   You breathe down their nostrils, through
your nose, just like horses do.   It usually works."

" How on earth do you learn all these secrets? " asked Robert.

" Dad showed me.   We just pass them on."

" Some of your ways must be ever so old."

" Yes.   Nobody knows where the Romanies came from.   Some
say Egypt and some say India.   We don't know ourselves."

They walked on in silence for a few minutes.   Robert was deep
in thought.   He wished he knew more about the Gypsies.   They
were almost as mysterious as the wild creatures.   He would love to
study their ways, and find out more about them.

Presently they reached an open space at the edge of a wood, and
Robert caught sight of the caravan.   It was painted bright green and
decorated with narrow lines and patterns of red.   Beside the caravan
sat two men and a woman hard at work.   Robert wondered what
they were making.   Luke took the wrapped fish from his pockets
and gave them to the woman without a word.   Then he gave Mr
Thornley's note to the older man and spoke a few words in his ear.
The man nodded and glanced at Robert.

" Nice morning," he said, and went on with his work.

" This way," said Luke, leading the way to the caravan.

Robert had always imagined that Gypsies were dirty, and he was
very surprised as he stepped inside the caravan.   The first thing he
noticed was the wide bed, which stretched right across the end of the

van. It was covered with a beautiful patchwork quilt, and the sheets were edged with snow-white lace. Just inside the door stood a brightly polished stove, with a tiny brass fender. Next to the stove was a built-in cupboard, and there was a seat under the window. Luke lifted the seat top, which was hinged, and Robert could see that it was the lid of a large locker.

On the other side of the van was a neat little corner-cupboard for china. A vase of flowers stood on the top, and there were two tiny brass rails to prevent it from sliding off. Next to this cupboard stood a chest of drawers, and then came another locker-seat. Everything looked perfectly clean and tidy.

" Where do you keep your odds and ends? " asked Robert.

" In the cratch," replied Luke, pointing to a deep shelf, which was built right across the van above the bed.

" What about food? "

" That's in the pan-box outside," replied Luke. He led the way down the steps and showed Robert a large cupboard which was fastened underneath the van.

" Well, what do you think of it? " asked Luke.

" It's super. I never imagined it would be like that. I wish I lived in a caravan."

" We call it a 'vardo '," said Luke.

" Sorry. I say, Luke, is it true that you have a secret language? "

" We used to have our own language years ago, but we don't use it much now. My old grandmother used to rakker Romanes."

" What does that mean? "

" That means talk in the Romany tongue."

At that moment one of the dogs gave a low growl, and looking up, Robert saw a man climbing over the fence into the lane. The man waved.

" It's Mr. Thornley," exclaimed Robert.

Luke's father raised his hand in reply, and rose to greet him as he approached. They shook hands. Robert noticed something unusual about the handshake, but he failed to notice what it was. The two men talked for a few minutes, using a number of strange words which Robert did not understand. Then Mr. Thornley turned to Robert.

" Well, Robert, did you enjoy your night out? "

" Yes, rather." Robert told Mr. Thornley about some of the things which they had seen, and about how Luke had retrieved the Captain's hunter. When he had finished, Mr. Thornley turned to Luke's father, who had gone back to his work.

" Can I give you a hand? " he asked.

Without a word the Gypsy handed him an old pair of scissors and pointed to some flattened biscuit tins which lay on the grass. Mr. Thornley sat down on a fallen tree beside the others, and started cutting the sheets of tin into narrow strips. Robert felt intensely curious.

" What is it you're making, Mr. Thornley? " he asked.

" Clothes-pegs. You watch Mr. Loveridge and you'll see the whole process."

Robert watched while Luke's father picked up a long stick of willow. He held a sharp knife in his left hand, and with his right hand he twirled the stick against the knife. The bark came curling off in long thin strips. His wife, who sat next to him, picked up the peeled sticks, one by one, and held each one over a stake which was

driven into the ground. She chopped each stick into short lengths, using a broken knife and a hammer.

Next to Luke's mother sat the young man. Robert guessed that he was Luke's elder brother. He was binding each length with a strip of tin, using nothing but a pair of pliers. Luke sat next to him, splitting the pegs with a knife and shaping the ends. He could not keep pace with the others, and presently his father left off peeling sticks and came to help him.

"Can I help?" asked Robert.

"Yes, my dear," replied Luke's mother. "You tie them up in dozens and put them in the basket."

Robert set to work. It seemed very strange, sitting there helping Gypsies to make pegs. He decided to take more interest in clothes pegs in future. Nobody spoke for some time. At length Mr Thornley began to talk about the tests he was making with the water vole and the hedgehog.

" Have you tried the urchin with an adder? " asked Luke's father.

" No, not yet. I thought maybe you could help me."

" Maybe," said the Gypsy, and they went on talking about other things. Robert's fingers were beginning to ache when Mr. Thornley rose and stretched.

" Time I was going," he said. He shook hands with Luke's father, while Luke turned to Robert.

" I'll be down by the river again tonight," he said.

" I'll be there," replied Robert.

" Come again," called Luke's mother, as they set off down the lane.

" Well, Robert, what do you think of Gypsies now? " asked Mr. Thornley, as they walked along the edge of Furnace Wood.

" I think they're jolly decent. That caravan—I mean that vardo —it was lovely inside. I had no idea they were like that."

" I expect you thought they were dirty."

" Yes. I didn't expect lace and brass and flowers in vases. They had a lovely quilt on the bed. I say, Mr. Thornley—do Gypsies have a special way of shaking hands? "

" Oh—so you noticed that, did you? "

" Yes. Will you show me how it's done? "

"Not yet. When you know them better, perhaps I will. That's a kind of secret pass-word. It wouldn't be fair to tell you yet."

"No, I suppose it wouldn't."

They walked on in silence until another question occurred to Robert.

"Do all Gypsies make clothes-pegs?" he asked.

"They do all sorts of things. Some of them make baskets and chairs, some sharpen knives and scissors, some are rat-catchers or mole-catchers, and most of them do some fruit-picking during the summer. Years ago Gypsies used to deal in horses, but horses are not used much now."

"Why don't they settle down and get proper jobs?"

"They love to be on the move, Robert. They wouldn't be happy if they had to settle."

As they walked along the edge of the wood they caught sight of the Keeper, some distance ahead. He waved to Mr. Thornley and vanished into the wood. The sight of the Keeper brought Robert's thoughts back to the subject of the poacher.

"I say, Mr. Thornley, what are you going to do about catching the poacher? We don't want the Gypsies to get the blame, do we?" he said.

"Don't worry, Robert," replied Mr. Thornley. "We've got a plan all worked out."

"I wish you would tell me what it is."

Mr. Thornley thought for a while before replying.

"That depends on whether you can keep a secret. If you talk, it will spoil everything."

" I can keep a secret. Besides, I want to help Luke and his family. I won't say a single word."

" Very well—this is the plan. The Loveridges will find the snares and inspect them early every morning. If the poacher really is the postman, he'll be at the Office sorting letters at that hour. In the meantime, I am going to send Jim a letter every day."

" Why? "

" Just to make sure that he calls at Jim's cottage every day."

" Why do you want him to do that? "

" Well, we think that he probably inspects his snares on his early rounds. Suppose he does. If he catches a bird, where do you think he hides it? "

" He could hide it in his post-bag."

" That's just what we think. Now this is how the plan will work. When there's a bird in a snare, the Gypsies will send me word. I shall then call on Jim, and be there when the postman arrives. It's just as well to have a witness."

" Yes, but how are you going to look inside his bag? You can't just order him to turn it out."

Mr. Thornley smiled.

" Quite right, Robert. That question puzzled us for some time, but Jim's wife found the answer."

" What was the answer? "

" I think I've said enough."

" I'd love to be there when it happens," said Robert.

" Perhaps that can be arranged. Now remember, not a word to anyone."

They looked over the fence at the fox's earth as they passed by, but all was quiet.   After leaving the edge of the wood they crossed a field and came out into the lane just beyond the Fisherman's Rest.

"Didn't you find an unusual nest in this lane the other day?" asked Mr. Thornley.

"Oh yes—the one with the cuckoo's egg."   Robert glanced up and down the lane, looking for a silver birch by which he had marked the spot.   When he had found it he led Mr. Thornley to the nest.

"You look first," said Mr. Thornley.   Robert peered through the leaves, but to his disappointment the eggs had gone.

"I can't see the eggs," he said.   "There's something black in the nest—Oh."   He backed out suddenly.

"What's the matter?" asked Mr. Thornley.

"They've hatched.   They opened their mouths when I touched them, and it made me jump."

Mr. Thornley looked into the nest.

"This is lucky," he said.

"They look about one

day old, and there's the cuckoo in the middle. Look—he's the one without the black down. I'll fix up my camera on the opposite bank, and try to get some pictures."

" Do you mean you'll actually watch the cuckoo throwing the babies out? " asked Robert.

" Yes. I'll take a moving picture if possible."

" I think baby cuckoos are cruel," said Robert. " If I were watching I should put the hedge-sparrows back."

" It wouldn't be much use, Robert. The cuckoo would only throw them out again."

" Why doesn't the mother bird put them back? "

" She doesn't appear to recognise them as her babies once they are out of the nest. Even if they are lying on the edge of the nest, she takes no more interest in them."

Robert shook his head.

" I think cuckoos are horrid birds," he said. " They should all be shot—like crows."

" You can't solve Nature's problems that way, Robert," said Mr. Thornley, as they walked down the hill. " If you decide to become a naturalist you will meet with many things which appear to be harsh. It's no use getting angry about them. We have to try to understand the reason for them."

Coffee was waiting for them when they arrived at the Fisherman's Rest. Robert felt terribly sleepy when he sat down.

" Did you do any more fishing after I left you last night? " asked Mr. Thornley.

" Yes, Luke showed me how to catch fish with a torch."

" You're not going to tell me you caught one that way."

" I did. It was the biggest one of all. We ate it for breakfast."

" Well done. I expect you were up early this morning, too."

" Yes. I saw the sun coming up over Furnace Wood. It looked lovely."

" That means you only had about six hours' sleep last night. Up to bed with you."

" Oh, Mr. Thornley——"

" Come along. No arguing."

Robert knew that was no use, so he went upstairs to lie down. The next thing he heard was the sound of the grandfather clock in the hall striking five.

CHAPTER XII

IN THE BAG

ROBERT had a good wash and came downstairs, to find an appetising high tea laid ready. There was ham, hard-boiled eggs, and salad. Tom Wickenden told him that Mr. Thornley was expected at any minute, and at a quarter past five Mr. Thornley walked in, carrying his camera.

" Hallo, Robert," he said. " Had a good sleep? "

" Too good, I think. Fancy sleeping all the afternoon, like a baby."

" Don't let that upset you. All good naturalists have to do it at times. You can't do good work if you are feeling sleepy."

" Did you get some good pictures? " asked Robert.

" Yes. I filmed the cuckoo while it threw out two of the babies, and I found a foster-mother for them."

" What do you mean? "

" I discovered a robin's nest with young ones about the same age, so I put the young hedge-sparrows into it."

" What will you do with the others? "

" There's a linnet's nest in the garden hedge, and her eggs hatched yesterday. I'll put them in there."

" Why does the young cuckoo throw the babies out? "

" Probably because if they remained there wouldn't be enough food for them."

In the Bag

" Well, how does the cuckoo know what to do?   It hasn't even
got its eyes open."

Mr. Thornley shook his head.

" I wish I knew the answer.   We call it instinct, but that doesn't
explain anything.   I say, that salad looks good.   I'll put my things
away, and be down in a minute."

They had just finished their tea when they heard a knock at the
door.   Tom Wickenden went to answer it, and returned looking
puzzled.

" It's a Gypsy boy, sir.   Says he wants you."

Mr. Thornley and Robert hurried to the door.   There stood Luke,
holding a wooden box, with a strip of leather attached for a handle.

" Something you wanted," he said.

" An adder? " asked Mr. Thornley.

Luke nodded, as if it were as simple a matter to fetch an adder as a
loaf of bread.

" Come in," said Mr. Thornley, " there's some cake inside."   He
gripped Luke's arm and led him into the dining-room.

" I say, how did you catch it? " asked Robert.   Luke smiled at
his surprise.

" Dad caught it.   He knew where to find one.   They lie out
in the sun when it's hot.   He just slipped a forked stick over its
head."

" Isn't it jolly difficult? "

" Not all that difficult.   You have to move pretty fast, but Dad's
done it lots of times.   Some Gypsies can handle adders without
being bitten."

Robert stared at him.

" It's true, pal. We call them Sapengro. That means snake master."

" That's quite right, Robert," said Mr. Thornley. " I saw it don once in the New Forest."

He turned to Luke, who was busily munching a large slice of cake

" What are your plans tonight, Luke? "

" I'm going fishing again," replied Luke. He glanced at Rober who quickly took the hint.

" Can I go with him, Mr. Thornley? " he asked.

" Very well—as long as you don't make a fuss about sleepin during the day. Are you still interested in fox-cubs? "

" Rather."

" If you hide at the bottom of Long Ride in Furnace Wood yo may see the vixen teaching them to hunt for mice."

" Did you see them there? "

" No, not this year. I noticed this morning that something ha been scratching up the turf just there, and I know that's a good plac for field-mice. They eat the beechmast. You'll see the mice ever if you don't see the foxes."

At that moment steps were heard in the passage. There came tap on the door, and Tom Wickenden looked in.

" The men are here, sir," he announced.

" Good. We're all ready. Come along, boys."

He picked up a basket from a corner, took the box from Luke and led the way to Bob Blake's garden, where a group of men wa waiting.

" Well, sir, what are you going to try them on this time? " aske Bob.

In the Bag

" I'd like to try the vole first.   I'm going to offer it eggs and meat
once more, just to prove that it isn't a rat.   I expect Tom has told
you that it didn't touch the chick."   He bent down and took from
his basket two pheasants' eggs and a small piece of raw steak, which
he placed in the tank.

" I shall have to put in some green stuff later on, or it will starve,"
he said.

" What kind of green stuff? " asked Robert.

" Willow, horsetail, flags, sedge, even grass.   They will eat nuts
and acorns too, but never eggs or chicks, in spite of what Tom
says."

" Well, sir, after seeing that bat I feel inclined to take your word
for it," said Tom.

Mr. Thornley turned to the hedgehog's tank.   From his basket he
took a small dish of bread and milk and two more pheasants' eggs.
" I'll try him with the eggs first, as Jim suggested," he said.
" I'll give him a drop of milk to fetch him out."

He poured a little milk into a saucer and lowered it into the tank,
laying a pheasant's egg beside it.   In a few moments the hedgehog
crept cautiously out of its den, its nose pointing this way and that.
It ran to the saucer and lapped up the milk.   Then it explored the
bottom of the tank, taking no notice of the egg.   Several times it
ran past it, and even touched it.

" Now watch," whispered Mr. Thornley.   He bent down,
picked up the egg, and cracked it against a stone, tipping the contents
into the saucer.   The hedgehog was startled by the movement and
curled up, but it soon resumed its search for food.   When it reached
the saucer it stopped at once and eagerly licked up the broken egg.

" What did I tell you . . ." growled Henry Martin.

" Wait a minute," said Mr. Thornley. " He didn't touch th
egg until it was broken. Whole eggs have lain there untouched a
night. Ask Tom."

" That means he only eats broken eggs," remarked George Good
sell. " He's doing you a favour, Henry—cleaning up your her
house."

" I'm not satisfied. You show me something really useful tha
he can do," grumbled Henry.

Mr. Thornley said nothing, but stooped and lifted Luke's littl
box.

" What is it now? Don't tell me they eat ferrets," exclaimed Ton

" No, it's not a ferret this time, Tom. It's something much mo
dangerous," replied Mr. Thornley. He unfastened the catch, hel
the box above the tank, and tipped it upside down. Out fell a larg
wriggling snake, and the men drew back their heads at the ur
expected sight.

" Goodness—it's an adder," exclaimed George Goodsell.

The adder glided round and round the tank, seeking some mear
of escape. The hedgehog, which had curled up, poked out the ti
of its nose. Robert noticed how the prickles stuck out forwar
over its face, like a spiky helmet.

Suddenly the adder noticed the hedgehog. It hissed and prompt
curled up, facing its enemy.

For a long time neither creature moved. Robert was afraid th
the men would get tired of waiting. At last the hedgehog began t
creep forward, step by step. The adder hissed again, and sudden
—" Whack ! "—it flung itself forward. Now Robert understoo

ow those tiny fangs could penetrate the skin, for behind them was
e whole weight of the snake's body. The hedgehog withdrew
s nose a little and stopped. It was not hurt, for the adder had struck
ly its prickles.

Suddenly the hedgehog darted forward and bit the adder near the
il. The adder struck again and again, hissing fiercely, and soon its
ead was bleeding from many wounds. The hedgehog attacked
ain. The snake continued to strike, but now it was becoming
chausted, and its movements were growing feebler. Finally the
edgehog grasped the adder close to its head and killed it. When
ceased to move, the hedgehog sniffed the body right down to the
il and began to eat it.

" What about that, Henry ? " asked Mr. Thornley.

Henry scratched his head.

" I'm not going to argue with you any more, sir. You know a
ght more than I do, that I'll say. I'd never have believed an urchin
uld do that."

" You won't kill them any more then ? "

" Not I—not after that. I remember how scared of snakes I used

to be when I was a little 'un.   If they kill snakes they're welcome
a broken egg now and then."

The other men murmured agreement.

"Well, boys, you can go off to your camp now," said M
Thornley.   "Take some bread and lard this time, Robert, and a fe
rashers, in case you have no luck with the fish.   Tom will get
ready for you."

When Robert's supplies were ready the boys set off.   The
walked along the river bank until they came to the hollow tre
where they hid their supplies.   Luke showed Robert a place whe
they could lie close to the water and watch the fish swim pa
They lay in the cool grass for a long time, fascinated by the sudd
movements of a shoal of tiny creatures which Luke said were bat
eels.   Once a long dark shape with a pointed snout glided past, an
Luke said it was a pike.

When they were tired of watching the fish they sat up.

"Like to try your hand at guddling?" asked Luke.

"What's that?"

"Catching fish in your hands by stroking them.   Some peop
call it tickling."

"Yes, I'd like to have a go."

Luke rose and led the way to the lower end of a broad still stret
of water.

"Always start at the lower end of the pool," he whispered.

"Why?"

"If you startle a fish it always runs downstream.   You dor
want it to warn the rest."

He leaned over the bank, looking closely at the water.

" Lie down here," he whispered. " Put your hand in gently and slide it forward under that big stone. Go slowly. If you feel a tail, pause a minute. Then start stroking the fish's belly. You must move your hand forwards, bit by bit. When you feel his gill-slits, get a grip with your finger and thumb, and hook him out."

Robert lay down and slid his arm into the water. It seemed silly to imagine that one could actually catch a fish with one's bare hands. He groped cautiously beneath the stone, and suddenly he felt something moving. Yes, it was a fish. In his excitement he moved his hand too quickly, and the fish shot away downstream.

" Stay there and try again," whispered Luke.

Robert waited for about five minutes, and slid his hand forward again. He felt another fish, and began stroking it as Luke had said. At last he reached the gently moving gill-covers, and gripped, but he was a fraction of a second too late. The fish slid clean through his fingers and escaped.

No more fish came, and Robert's arm began to ache with the coldness of the water. Presently Luke gave the signal to move, and they made their way upstream to a fresh place. This time they lay down behind a screen of alders. Robert groped gently beneath a large slippery stone, but he felt nothing. He was about to whisper to Luke when he noticed strong ripples heaving the still surface of the water, and a dark blunt head appeared close to the opposite bank. An otter! It swam towards a bush which hung down over the water, and now Robert could see a hole under the bush. Something was moving in the hole. The otter had landed now and was crawling out of the water. Robert could see a fish in her mouth, and he could see three little heads moving in the mouth of the burrow.

The large otter pushed her nose in beneath the overhanging brambles, and then seemed to change her mind; she suddenly turned and dived, and Robert heard the cubs whine. The mother appeared again about a yard from the bank, still holding the fish. One cub stretched his nose out so far that he fell in, but he promptly turned and scrambled out. The mother hung motionless in the water for about a minute, waiting for the cubs to swim, but they were evidently not brave enough. Presently she glided forward under the bush, and Robert had a glimpse of the cubs dragging the fish up into the burrow. The mother sank out of sight, and only a ripple marked the way she went.

Robert turned round to face Luke.

" I say—did you see that? "

Luke nodded, his eyes still fixed on the spot.

" I guessed she had a holt somewhere round here. No wonder the fish are nervous. I'd like to see her teach the cubs to swim. My Dad says she pushes them in."

The boys waited for a long time, but there was no further sign of the otter. Shadows began to creep across the meadow, and the air grew cool.

" I don't suppose she'll come again till it's dark," said Luke. " What about looking for the foxes? "

" Right-oh," replied Robert.

They crept quietly away and set off towards Furnace Wood. Climbing the gate very carefully, to avoid making any noise, they walked softly up the path till they reached a spot where it joined a broad ride. Here they noticed a fallen tree, surrounded with bracken, which would serve for a hide. They settled down behind he trunk, watching the broad ride, which appeared to be quite deserted.

Robert listened to the birds singing their evening songs, and wondered if Mr. Thornley were right about the reason for their singing. They sound so happy, he thought. He wished they would sing all the year round. Everything was so still that Robert felt like dozing. Then a rabbit hopped across the ride, on its way down to the meadow. Another appeared, and another, till there was a steady trickle of rabbits. Some sat very still listening, and then put their noses down to nibble the turf.

Suddenly a blackbird shrieked out its chattering alarm, and the rabbits bolted. Something's coming, thought Robert—perhaps it's the poacher. He hoped it wasn't. He could hear a faint rustling now, but it didn't sound like human footsteps. Something was moving under the hazels across the ride. Then out walked a small plump fox-cub. It looked up and down the ride, cocking its big pointed ears. Robert could even see its whiskers twitching.

Next moment the vixen glided out from the undergrowth, lean and suspicious. Robert could see her cunning yellow eyes as she glanced about her. It seemed impossible that she should fail to notice the boys, but Luke had chosen the spot carefully, and the slight breeze was blowing their scent downhill. Two more cubs followed her, and they all stood in the ride looking up and down, twitching their ears at the slightest sound.

When the vixen was satisfied that all was clear, she lowered her head and began sniffing the turf. She moved slowly along the ride, the cubs following and watching her closely. Suddenly she pressed her nose down into the turf and made a pounce with her

front paws. Then she shook her head like a terrier and tossed some
thing aside. The cubs rushed to seize it and scuffled for it. Th
vixen went on sniffing, and the cubs began to copy her. Th
animals moved slowly away down the ride until they were los
among the deepening shadows.

All was still. A tawny owl began to hoot, and his sinister ca
echoed through the trees as it would in a great cathedral. As th
sound died away, a loud rustle in the dead leaves made Robert star
and he glimpsed a field-mouse dashing into its hole about a yar
from his foot. In a few seconds it popped out again, and bega
to run rapidly about in search of something. It stopped close t
Luke's boot and sat up on its hind legs to nibble, holding a tiny beec
nut in its delicate hand-like paws. It looked so dainty that it re
minded Robert of a picture of a fairy, which he had seen in an illus
trated copy of *A Midsummer Night's Dream*.

Presently Luke stretched his leg, and the mouse vanished.

" We'd better be turning in, pal," he said.

" We've seen some interesting things tonight, haven't we? " said
.obert, as they made their way slowly through the shadowy wood.

" Yes. You don't usually see as much in one evening. You
1ust be lucky."

When they reached the tent they lit a fire and fried some bacon
nd bread. Robert thought they should have saved the bacon for
reakfast, but Luke promised to be up early and catch some fish.
'hey sat for a while in the firelight, listening to the cries of birds and
1e rippling water.

" I wish I could always live like this," said Robert.

When the fire died down they decided to turn in. Robert did
ot notice the hardness of the ground, and in a very few minutes he
vas fast asleep.

·   ·   ·   ·

Luke was shaking his shoulder, but Robert felt terribly sleepy.

" What's the matter? " he mumbled.

" Wake up. We've got to warn John Thornley," said Luke,
;iving him another shake.

" Oh dear. What's happening? " groaned Robert. " Surely
t isn't time to get up." He sat up wearily, and looked round at a
lim, grey landscape, shrouded with mist.

" It's the poacher," explained Luke. " There's a couple of birds
n the snares. Dad just came round to tell me."

" What's the time? " asked Robert.

" It's gone five."

Robert crawled out of his sleeping-bag and shivered. The air

felt cold. He sat wearily on the bag, tying up his shoes, wonderin
if he were still asleep and dreaming, while Luke stood waiting.

"Come on, pal," he said. "You'll feel better when we g
going. You're not as used to it as we are."

Robert realised that the birds were singing, and he began to chee
up. They walked through the wet grass towards the Fisherman's Res
Mallard duck were rising in groups from the misty water, and moo
hens were swimming jerkily for cover. Robert noticed a numbe
of rabbits sitting out at the edge of the wood, staring as thoug
they could not believe that human beings could be about so early.

They climbed the stile into the lane, and soon their feet crunche
loudly on the gravel path beneath Mr. Thornley's window.

"I say, how are we going to wake him?" asked Robert.

Luke stooped, and picking up a handful of gravel, he tossed it u
against the panes. In a few moments Mr. Thornley's head appeare

"Any news, boys?" he asked.

"A couple of birds in the snares," replied Luke.

"Right. I'll be down in a minute. Wait at the back door."

They walked round to the back door. Soon they heard the bolt
being moved, and the door opened.

"Come in," said Mr. Thornley. "Don't make a noise. Ton
isn't up yet. Sit by the stove, and we'll have a cup of cocoa."

Robert sat down gratefully beside the stove. Mr. Thornle
raised the hot-plate cover and set a pan of milk to warm while h
went upstairs to dress. In a few minutes he returned and prepare
the cocoa. The comforting warmth and the sight of the steamin
cup made Robert feel more cheerful.

"What's going to happen, Mr. Thornley?" he asked.

" We must get to Jim's cottage before the postman calls. He generally calls just before seven. We'd better start early, so that we can give Jim plenty of warning."

" Yes, but what are we going to do? Are we going to arrest the poacher? "

" We can't do that. This isn't a Wild West film. We're simply going to find out if he's got the birds on him."

" What do you want us to do? "

" Luke had better hide. If the postman sees him he may get suspicious. You can come and watch."

" I wish Luke could watch too."

" I expect I shall have a job for Luke. Well, are we ready? "

They talked very little as they walked through the fields to Jim's cottage. As they arrived they saw Jim coming out of the gate with buckets of food for his young birds, and the two men talked quietly together. Then Jim went on with his work as though nothing was happening.

" Luke, you hide in the woodshed. He'll leave his bike in the lane at the back, and walk across the field. Keep watch from the window, and give me a whistle as soon as you see him. Robert, you come with me."

Mr. Thornley led the way into the kitchen, where the Keeper's wife was preparing breakfast.

How the time dragged! Robert thought it would never pass, but at last he heard Luke's warning whistle. Jim was washing his hands at the sink, and he came in and sat down. Robert caught a glimpse of the postman's cap passing the window, and then came a tap at the door.

" Come in," called the Keeper.

" Morning, Jim," said the postman as he entered, letter in hand
" You're getting a lot of post lately."

" Aye—more catalogues I expect," replied the Keeper.

"Will you have a cup of tea? " asked the Keeper's wife.

" Thanks," replied the postman. " This is getting quite a habit.'
He dumped his bag in the corner close to the kitchen-range, and sa
down. As he did so, he noticed Mr. Thornley.

" Morning, sir. Up early this morning," he said.

" I'm often about early," replied Mr. Thornley.

The Keeper's wife lifted the teapot and put it down again.

" We'll need a drop of hot water," she said.

" Pass it over to me," said Mr. Thornley. " I can reach the
kettle."

All this time Robert was feeling quite bewildered. Why didn'
Mr. Thornley say something about the pheasants? Weren't they
going to do anything? Then he noticed that the Keeper's mouth
was set in a tight line, and his hands were trembling. Something
exciting was going to happen.

Mr. Thornley poured some boiling water into the teapot, but a
he did so his fingers slipped. The pot tipped sideways, the lid fel
off with a clatter, and hot tea poured down on to the postman'
bag.

" My goodness—your letters will be ruined! " cried the Keeper
He grasped the bag and tipped it upside down.

" No! No! " cried the postman, jumping to his feet, but it wa
too late. A pile of letters fell out on to the floor, and in the middle
lay two plump pheasants.

Everyone stared at the postman, and for several seconds there was tense silence.

" Well—how do you explain this? " asked the Keeper angrily.

" It's the Gypsies," replied the postman. " I caught them in the ane with those birds this morning."

" Oh, you did, did you? Where were you taking them? "

" I was taking them to the Captain, of course."

" Why didn't you give them to me? "

" Well, if you must know, I thought he might give me a reward or them."

" Hm. That's a likely tale," said the Keeper.

" That's my story, and I'm sticking to it," replied the postman. ' You can't disprove it. It's no use asking the Gypsies. Everyone knows they can't be trusted."

The Keeper glanced at Mr. Thornley. He did not know what t
do next.

" We can't just let it go at that," said Mr. Thornley. " We'
send the Captain word about what's happened, and we'll see yo
later. What time do you finish your round? "

" Ten-thirty. You can see me after that at the Office, though
don't see what good it will do." The postman picked up his lette:
and departed without another word.

" The cunning rascal! " exclaimed the Keeper. " I don't see ho
we can prove anything if he sticks to that story."

" Don't worry, Jim, everything's under control," replied M
Thornley. " Just meet me at the Post Office at ten-thirty."

He hurried out to the woodshed, followed by Robert. Luke w
still waiting inside the shed.

" Luke, you go straight back to the vardo," said Mr. Thornley
" Tell your Dad that we've found the birds, and he's to meet us
ten-thirty at the Post Office. Tell him it's important." Luk
hurried away, and Mr. Thornley turned to Robert, who was st
looking perplexed.

" Don't worry, Robert—I guessed this might happen," h
said.

" Yes, but how can we prove that it wasn't the Gypsies? They'
get the blame for it now."

" No, they won't. I met the Captain the other night, and tol
him all about our plan. He thought it was a good idea, and h
arranged for Mr. Loveridge to go straight to the Hall and tell him a
soon as anything was found in the snares."

" I still don't see how we can prove who did it."

" Well, there's one satisfaction—the Gypsies won't get the blame for it."

They walked back to the Fisherman's Rest and had breakfast. Then Mr. Thornley went to his room to do some writing, and Robert waited. How slowly the hands of the clock seemed to move. Several times he thought it had stopped. After what seemed like a whole morning the clock struck ten, and Mr. Thornley appeared.

" Come along, Robert—let's go," he said.

As they approached the little Post Office, Robert noticed a policeman standing on the opposite side of the street. They went through into a small inner room, where the postman sat reading a newspaper. He glanced up at them and went on reading. Footsteps sounded outside and in walked the Captain, followed by Jim. The postman looked up again and laid his paper down.

" Hurry up with your questions," he said rudely, " I want to be getting home."

The Captain flushed angrily and squared his shoulders.

" Stand up ! " he snapped. The postman looked surprised, but after a moment's hesitation he stood up.

" Now, my man, I want the truth," said the Captain. " Have you been poaching on my land ? "

" No, sir. It's the Gypsies. I was bringing the birds to you," replied the postman.

" I'll give you one more chance to admit your guilt," said the Captain grimly. " Do you admit it ? "

" No, I do not. It's the Gypsies, I tell you."

" Very well," said the Captain. He walked across to the door.

" Come in," he said, and in walked Mr. Loveridge, the groom and the policeman, followed by Luke.

" Officer," said the Captain, " I wish to charge this man with poaching."

" Yes, sir. Any witnesses, sir? "

" Certainly. My groom, Mr. Loveridge, and myself."

" What—you, sir? " exclaimed the surprised policeman.

" Quite correct. I had word brought to me early this morning that some game was caught in a snare in my woods, so the three of us kept watch. This man removed the birds from a snare. We all saw him."

" That's right, Constable," said the groom, and Mr. Loveridge nodded in agreement. Robert stared in astonishment, and even Mr. Thornley looked surprised.

" Well, Mr. Turner, I'm afraid I shall have to take you in charge," said the policeman. He took the astonished postman by the arm and led him out, followed by the witnesses.

" Gosh—what a surprise ! " cried Robert. He put his arm round Luke's shoulder and hugged him in his excitement.

" That was a surprise to me," confessed Mr. Thornley. " Fancy the Captain getting up at that hour, and going out to watch for poachers."

" He's a sport," said Robert. " I say, Mr. Thornley, what will they do with the postman? Will they send him to prison? "

" I doubt it. I expect he'll get a fine. The main thing is that he's been exposed, and won't be able to blame others for his misdeeds. I think this calls for a little celebration. Come across to the sweet shop, and choose what you like."

After their celebration Robert and Mr. Thornley returned to the

Fisherman's Rest. Mr. Thornley reminded Robert that his holiday was nearly over, and Robert looked so sad that Mr. Thornley suggested another visit at Whitsun.

" I don't know whether Dad will agree," said Robert. " I wish I could find out. Then I might arrange to meet Luke again."

" We can soon settle that," said Mr. Thornley. " I'll ring him up."

Robert waited anxiously while Mr. Thornley telephoned, and after a lot of delay they heard Mr. Armstrong's voice.

" Yes, he can come again. It's an education for him. You arrange it with the landlord. Are you having a nice quiet time?"

" Not exactly quiet. We've just helped to catch a poacher. Hold on—let Robert tell you about it." He handed the telephone to Robert, who gave his father a brief account of their adventure.

Robert felt more cheerful after this, and spent the rest of the morning in a hide watching squirrels with Mr. Thornley. After dinner he was glad to lie down and sleep for an hour. He came down for tea wondering how he could get in touch with Luke. Just then he heard a knock on the door, and there stood Luke himself.

" Hallo, Luke. Are you going fishing tonight?" asked Robert.

" Not tonight, pal. Dad sent a message asking you and John Thornley to come to the vardo. Come at about seven. We've got a surprise for you."

" Thank you," said Mr. Thornley, who had come to the door at the sound of Luke's voice. " We'll be there."

Just before seven o'clock they set off to visit the Gypsies. When they approached the vardo Robert noticed a pleasant smell of cooking, and saw Luke's mother busily stirring a large iron pot. They sat down, and were handed dishes of tender stewed meat, with potatoes and vegetables. This was followed by cold apple-pie, and after this came nuts and fruit, with drinks all round.

Robert could not help wondering where all the good things came from, and presently Luke explained.

" The Captain sent this stuff," he said. " He brought it round in his car."

" Was it really your Dad whom he knew in Burma? "

" Yes, it was. He was so pleased with us that he's given us permission to catch rabbits on his land, and he's promised to buy a New Forest pony next time we're up this way."

" That was jolly good of him," said Robert. " I say, Luke—do you think he might give your Dad a job? "

Luke shook his head.

" He offered him one, but Dad wouldn't take it. He's too fond of the road. We shall be moving on in a few days."

" So shall I. I've got to go back to London. I hope I shall see you again. It's going to be difficult to meet you if you're always on the move."

" Don't worry, pal. You give me your address and I'll send you a card when I'm up this way again. I'm not much of a hand at writing, but I can just about manage that."

" I shall be here again at Whitsun," said Robert.

" Good. We shall be here then for the fruit-picking. We'll do some more fishing and camping out, eh, pal? "

" I shall look forward to that," replied Robert.

Printed in Great Britain by Richard Clay and Company, Ltd., Bungay, Suffolk.